Also by Lorri Horn

Dewey Fairchild, Parent Problem Solver

DEWEY FAIRCHILD,

TEACHER PROBLEM SOLVER

Lorri Horn

Amberjack Publishing

New York | Idaho

AMBERJACK
PUBLISHING

Amberjack Publishing
1472 E. Iron Eagle Drive
Eagle, ID 83616
http://amberjackpublishing.com

Publisher's Cataloging-in-Publication data
Names: Horn, Lorri, author.
Title: Dewey Fairchild, teacher problem solver / by Lorri Horn.
Description: Eagle, ID : Amberjack Publishing, [2018] | Summary:
While sixth-grader Dewey is trying to help schoolmates solve their
teacher problems, the school itself enacts bizarre changes that lead
Dewey and his friends to commit acts some would call vandalism.
Identifiers: LCCN 2018006336 (print) | LCCN 2018014295
(ebook) | ISBN 9781944995867 (eBook) | ISBN 9781944995850
(hardcover : alk. paper)
Subjects: | CYAC: Middle schools--Fiction. | Schools--Fiction. |
Teachers--Fiction. | Humorous stories.
Classification: LCC PZ7.1.H664 (ebook) | LCC PZ7.1.H664 Dew
2018 (print) | DDC [Fic]--dc23
LC record available at https://lccn.loc.gov/2018006336

Cover Design & Illustrations: Agnieszka Grochalska

To Mom, my first democratic teacher.

And to all the amazing teachers who foster within children a sense of intellectual and emotional compassion, curiosity, and critical thinking regarding themselves, their environment, their community, and their world.

One named Bryan makes especially good husband material, too.

"I believe that education is the fundamental method of social progress and reform."

—John Dewey

The Miracle

Her mouth twisted to the right, and her lips pursed when she spoke. "Missus DECORDAAAYYY," she had told Bryan Frenchie and the other students that first day of class, her Humpty-Dumpty head bobbling gently up and down as if attached to her body with a spring. Mrs. Décorder had short flaming-red hair and wore Revlon's Candy Apple Red lipstick that smudged on her teeth. It always looked to Bryan like she'd taken a bite out of someone's arm or something.

When she spoke, it sounded like she was working half an apple slice around in her mouth. Vowels pooled on the back of her tongue and became three syllables long, consonants got caught between her teeth and lips. It's not that the kids couldn't understand what she said.

They just couldn't understand why she spoke that way. They all persisted in calling her Mrs. DEE-CORD-ERR.

Bryan and his best friend Ryan had been friends since kindergarten. There were plenty of ways to tell them apart. Bryan had short, wavy brown hair that arched heart-shaped over his eyebrows and rose a couple inches above his head. A nose, a bit large, sat squarely in the middle of his handsome suntanned face, and big, brown doe eyes belied hints of him being a goof-off. Ryan stood about the same height as his partner in crime, but appeared a good inch or so shorter due to his stick-straight, dark-brown hair that stuck flat against his head. His bangs lie plastered unevenly like piano keys across his creamy brow, perhaps a promise of the talented piano player he would one day become.

Nope, despite their common Anglo-Saxon forbearers, they looked nothing like one another. But, just as some kids mix up words like "principal" and "principle," poor Mrs. Décorder, who taught all the fifth-grade science classes, just couldn't keep Bryan and Ryan straight. She'd call Bryan, Ryan, and Ryan, Bryan. It became amusing for them to mix her up, and they'd confuse Mrs. Décorder with an endless loop of her calling Bryan by his correct name and Bryan telling her, "No, Mrs. Deecorderr, I'm Ryan," and Ryan telling her, "No, Mrs. Deecorderr, I'm Bryan," until finally, she became so befuddled she just bunched their names together as one. "Ryanandbryan, are you paying attention?" she'd ask. Or, "Ryanandbryan, please hand in your homework from last night."

Today, Ryanandbryan and the rest of the class prepared to watch a movie all about babies, called "The Miracle of Birth." Tech-savvy would not be counted among Mrs. Décorder's many attributes. To help her, she had created a list on the board of what she called "Tech-No-Helpers." Ryanandbryan found it comical that she spelled it that way and felt it left their level of assistance open to interpretation. Each week, it would be one student's turn to set up the SMART Board, get the laptops working, or turn off the lights—"Thomas Edison being one of our earliest tech-no innovators," she'd thrum. "Ryanandbryan" topped the list this week, and since Ryan had already had his turn, Bryan's arrived today.

"Ryanandbryan, can you please turn off the lights and get our film going?" Mrs. Décorder's voice sounded a hundred years old to them, though the difference between fifty-five and one hundred was pretty incidental.

Mrs. Décorder always, without fail, had on a white blouse, and she usually wore long, brightly colored slacks. Today she had chosen forest green, which accentuated her long legs. Bryan thought she looked like one of those inflatable moving advertisements made from long green and white fabric tubes as she flailed her arms around, gesturing above at the lights.

He got up from his seat, turned off the light, and set up the "film".(Mrs. Décorder always used such old school terminology).

He couldn't explain the source of his inspiration when Dewey Fairchild later asked, only that it seemed too good an idea not to do. It was the miracle of a baby being born. And Bryan played it—backwards.

Mrs. Décorder sat at her desk grading papers while the students watched aghast as the baby made its magical journey—that's right—into its mother instead of out! Their stunned silence quickly moved into laughter. Wes laughed so hard that he fell to the floor clutching his sides, and Ynez had tears streaming down her cheeks. If each kid had a control button, it was at full volume. The room sounded like the complete explosion of sound that only the many voices together can create.

"Ryanandbryan! Now, stop that! No, no. Now, I'll have to get you in trouble for that." Her long green legs strode over, and her head was in full bobble throttle as her extended finger wagged.

"Play that the correct direction, young man." As she spoke her warning, the piece of invisible apple tumbled around in her mouth.

She hurried to the screen and tripped on the area carpet, her long green bean legs splayed like a peace sign on the ground. "Ryanandbryan. You fix that," she admonished again. Bryan moved to comply, but not before he realized that if he moved the projector just a few baby inches over, Mrs. Décorder, still spread out on the carpet, could assume the role—of the screen! The class burst out again in an uproarious laughter as the projection of the baby now appeared on their teacher's back. As she slowly put her hands on her long legs and bent over to get back up, things got worse before they got better. When she finally regained her composure, Mrs. Décorder's hair looked like a red umbrella blown inside out after a windstorm. "Ryanandbryan, now, you let that baby come back out!"

Bryan played "The Miracle of Birth" the right way, but it was too late. No one paid any attention because nothing seemed more miraculous than what Bryan had just done.

Out

When Mrs. Décorder spoke, each word carried about 1.55 seconds per word—1.55285714285 to be precise. Bryan had timed her one day and taken an average. 1.55 seconds per word may not sound like a lot, but 1.55 seconds per word in a sentence of fifteen words dragged on, slowing everything down like gum stuck to the bottom of your shoe.

1.42

1.71

1.55

1.86

1.48

1.33

1.52

Without Bryan and Ryan, no one would have made it through a day. But try telling that to his mother or the principal. Once again, Bryan had landed in her office, trying to explain his "unsuitable behavior."

His principal, Mrs. Thais, believed in being fair-minded when it came to children, but she had grown tired of seeing this particular pair of boys in her office. Today, in her doorway, stood Bryan. Tomorrow, it would be Ryan.

She motioned Bryan with her eyes and chin to come in as she finished up a call. Still speaking as the long cord on her phone followed her around to the other side of her desk, she cradled the receiver on her shoulder and walked one chair from the wall and slid another from under a round table. She set the chairs across from one another.

"Sit, sit," she directed, pointing again with her chin as she spoke. "No, no," she continued her phone call laughing. "A student. Right. Okay. Tomorrow should work just fine." She hung up and flipped open the pages of a calendar.

"Just a minute," she said to Bryan. "If I don't write this down now, I'll never remember."

Bryan watched her turn the pages of her calendar. Mrs. Thais had a lot of lines on her forehead, and as she concentrated he thought of the smooth raked lines in the sand of the Zen Rock Garden at the Golden Gate Park.

She sat before him today, as she appeared every other day, her grey hair streaked with ribbons of black in a tight bun on her head. A pair of reading glasses nestled in her bun, and another pair peeked out of her breast pocket, like a pair of birds in their nests. She always wore a well-made suit jacket and a skirt. Today it was powder blue and accentuated her violet eyes which had read more books than Bryan could imagine if he'd ever bothered to wonder about such things about his principal. The walls around them were lined with a small fraction of them. Her office had a couch, a round table, the chairs they sat on now, and her big desk. Framed artwork painted by children hung on her walls.

"Mr. Frenchie," she sighed, smoothing out her skirt and sitting down. She also managed to smile now that she could give him her full focus. Despite how he and Ryan tired her, they really weren't bad kids. "Would you be so kind as to read to me Mrs. Décorder's referral, and then explain to me, in your own words, today's particular transgression?" She handed him the paper. Bryan fidgeted about in his chair a bit and first read to himself:

"Student Name: Ryanandbryan." She doesn't even learn my real name for the paperwork?! He knew better than to say anything about it at this moment.

He began aloud, "Reason for Referral: Ryanandbryan determined it best to run the class film on how babies are miraculously born, backwards. The infant went in instead of out, upsetting several of the children and making many others laugh for the duration of the film."

He looked up, trying hard not to smile.

"So then?" she asked, prompting him to address the issue at hand.

"Um, well, it says that I played the movie in the wrong direction, and that it disrupted the class."

"That's right. And while you've caused a disruption many times over your short career in room 32D, I must say that this is one of your more unsuitable moments of conduct."

It was some of my finest work, thought Bryan to himself. How he'd come up with the idea of reversing that baby's trajectory on the spot seemed nothing short of sheer genius!

"Let me make it as simple and clear as possible for you," continued Principal Thais, interrupting his reverie, "one more transgression and you're out."

Out. Bryan didn't know what that meant, but he felt his face flush. Out of chances? Out for the day? The week? His whole life? He could tell by her tone that she meant business though, and he thought better than to ask any questions for fear of what she might say.

"Do you have any questions?" she asked, hands on her hips as she stood up and looked down at him.

"N-n-no, Mrs. Thais." He looked her directly in her eyes to show that he was paying attention.

As he walked out of her office and down the hallway, he regained his composure, but he knew he needed help. And he knew just where he should go to get it.

Teacher Problem Solver

Dewey's backpack weighed a ton. He started the year with five separate three-ring binders, and each class had a heavy textbook. He managed to reduce it down to three binders, but it still probably weighed about fifty pounds and felt like he carried around a backpack full of bricks. It didn't matter how many times his parents picked it up and declared it too heavy for his growing back—it didn't get any lighter. They wanted him to use one of those rolling backpacks, but he wouldn't be caught dead with one of those. You couldn't just throw them on your back and run with them.

He still wore his thick camel-brown straight hair below his ears. Maybe it was a bit longer this year in what his mother called a California-messy boy way. That was more about not bothering to get a haircut though. He'd never liked to wear his hair showing his ears, and he certainly wasn't going to start in sixth grade. He must have grown taller because his parents' friends said stuff like, "Oh my goodness! He's a full head taller!" He hadn't really noticed that himself, though he did stand taller than Colin by about an inch now. His mom complained that he outgrew his Vans before he wore them out. She'd started having his dad buy them on eBay, which meant that he'd ended up with a pair of slip-ons, so he took over searching for them himself. This fall began with a pair of the Authentics with laces in navy blue. He begged his dad to sell the slip-ons.

Tons of new kids he'd never even met filled the classrooms and hallways. That could be good for business, but Dewey got this dull empty feeling inside with so many faces in class he didn't know and the bigger crowds during lunch and break. He and Colin both had Humanities together, and Seraphina shared Spanish class with him again, but otherwise, the only class they had together was study hall. He had new teachers, a new campus, lockers, vending machines. Vending Machines! Snacks on demand! Now, *there* was an improvement over elementary school.

This afternoon though, he'd left his backpack behind. He was sitting in his office, conveniently and secretly, located in his attic. His desk and chair sat just where and how he'd left them. Clara, although she didn't live there, sat already waiting for him too, with a warm plate of cookies and her eighteen-pound black-and-white Havanese dog, Wolfie.

"I just don't understand the entire Snapchat concept," Clara was saying. "You post it and it disappears?"

Clara sat on the floor with a pile of papers before her. To look at Clara Cottonwood and try to determine her age would be a lot like looking at a tree in the forest. Without the benefit of counting its ninety-four rings, you'd hardly know more than that it stood solid and grand.

"Well, it stays there ten seconds."

"Ten seconds? What's the point of that?" asked Clara. She stood up with ease, a full four-foot-nine-inches tall, and lowered the blinds to block the sun shining directly in their eyes.

"That's just how it works. It's just meant to be there for a sec. People don't have to worry about what they post that way because it just goes away."

"Hmm," Clara sounded suspicious as she moved to join him again on the floor. She'd been trying to recreate all their files as hard copies on paper so they'd have a backup of all their work. As she sat, she pulled her soft cotton, grey pants gently just above her knees to make room to sit. She wore a turtle neck today, which accentuated the neat grey bun on her head. The papers all over the floor were a mess, but not a hair stuck out of place. Dewey could feel in that "hmm" that she felt dissatisfied with his explanation.

"You know," Dewey reassured, her slate grey eyes holding his own, "you can do random stuff that doesn't matter cause it's just going to disappear."

"Like what?" she arched her eyebrow.

"Just like hanging out with friends. Or a picture of Wolfie. Come here, Boy!" He took a shot of Wolfie, with his pink tongue sticking out and curled up against his black button nose like a strawberry fruit roll up and wrote, "hmu if you love."

"Oh, I see!" Clara smiled warmly at the picture of Wolfie, appreciating his white bushy brows jutting out like an old man's over his soft marble-black eyes. Clara loved how he had the little white fur around his mouth and how his chest and front paws were silky snow white against his black body and those crazy white brows. Evidently others appreciated this charm as well, as Dewey's phone kept vibrating with all the "love."

"But the bigger thing is that all these clients chatted me their info. So now it's just gone, poof. It's not like regular texts 'cause these delete instantly."

"And let me guess," Clara remarked. "Some people chat stuff they don't want saved."

"Right!" encouraged Dewey. "No one texts anymore 'cause no one gives out their numbers. You don't even need a user name for Snapchat, just a picture to add. See? Get it?"

She looked over his shoulder, smiling at a picture someone else had sent him of their own dog's tongue sticking out.

"Oh, I get it. I get that there's no way in carnation to keep up with this in our record-keeping," she shrugged at him and then looked around for Wolfie. "Wolfie! Wolfie! Where'd he go?" He had run off with a sheet of paper and shredded it up for entertainment. "Wolfie! Argh! Hippity hop, dog! Come on! Let's go out for a wee."

"Ha! Maybe paper isn't all that easier to keep track of!" laughed Dewey. "I *can* save the chats. I just have to remember to do that," suggested Dewey.

"Chances of that?" asked Clara, lifting Wolfie up as Dewey quickly snapped a picture of them and posted it on Snapchat with the caption, "In the doghouse."

"I can do it, but it sounds awful. Why do we have to keep track of it all, anyway?"

"*Tbh*, I don't know," she shrugged.

Before he could ask her how she knew what *tbh*

meant, and before she and Wolfie could head up and out to conduct his business, Bryan Frenchie came careening down the slide and onto the lofty 700 fill power Hungarian goose-down pillow landing-pad. Dewey knew Bryan from last year, when Bryan was in fourth grade, and Dewey had been in fifth.

"Oh, hey Bryan! What brings you here?" Dewey asked as Wolfie freed himself, flounced over, and put his head down into the landing-pad, indicating to Bryan that he required his greeting in the form of a back rub. Bryan missed the cue though and instead clumsily patted Wolfie a few times on the head and squashing it head down deeper into the pillow. Wolfie surfaced with his face looking like a mushed peanut butter sandwich, and Clara gave a chuckle.

Momentarily distracted, Bryan cocked his own head in a sort of *well-isn't-that-an-interesting-look* kind of way and then answered Dewey, "I'm in trouble. I'm going to get myself kicked out of class or school or something. I'm pretty sure I need your help."

Dewey, who, over the past couple of years, had established himself to be none other than the greatest parent problem solver, logically assumed that Bryan meant for him to help him with his parents on this issue and handed him the standard paperwork to fill out, which asked the requisite questions about the problems the client's parents cause and best hiding places in the home and workplace.

"No, you don't understand," clarified Bryan looking up from the paperwork. "My parents aren't the problem. Not yet, anyway! My teacher is."

Dewey and Clara looked at each other with interest. This was new. A teacher problem. *Well, why not?* thought Dewey. *How different can it really be?*

"What's the basic problem?" asked Dewey, reorienting himself.

"The problem is she's a nut job, and I'm having too much fun."

"So what's the issue again? I'm not totally getting it. Why would that be a problem?"

"I think, sir," clarified Clara, "Mr. Bryan is concerned that she's driving him to entertain himself and others, and for that, if I'm understanding correctly, he, not she, is being reprimanded."

"Yes, yes, that's it!"

Without missing more than another beat and a half, Dewey replied, "Ah, right. Teacher problems. That's a different day," Dewey confirmed, covering for the fact that he hadn't expected this as a topic at all. "We see those issues *tomorrow*." Clearly, he needed to stall. "Can you come back tomorrow, Bryan? We will be glad to take your case and work with you then."

Bryan nodded yes, but his shoulders sagged just the tiniest bit as he stood up. Clara handed him two warm sugar cookies wrapped in a napkin and gave him three small, gentle pats on his back. This time, instead of climbing on Clara's back to get up to the air ducts, as clients of the past had done, they showed Bryan to a platform and had him step on it. Dewey pressed a button, and it lifted Bryan up to the air ducts so that he could climb back out the way he'd come into the attic.

The idea of installing the Garage Gator Electric Motorized Lift System as a mini-elevator for his clients had been Colin's. The installation went easily, or so Clara reported. The kit came with its one 3/4" drill bit and would hold up to 170 pounds—a nice addition to their operation, as well as a good idea with Clara's back starting to feel the weight of how busy they'd become.

Dewey called out into the air ducts to be sure Bryan was no longer in earshot, and then he spoke.

"Teacher Problem Solver! Fascinating. We can do that, right, Clara? I am sure we can do that. It's not all that different. We just gotta change a few lines on the paperwork is all!"

Clara pulled up the usual form: "Name? Grade? School?" Clara read.

"Well, all of that is helpful," replied Dewey. "Go on."

"Home Address?"

"Keep that. Why not? But better add school address as well," and Clara revised.

"Best Entry to Your Home Without Being Noti—"

"Ah! Yes, that part is going to prove trickier, isn't it? Delete that. We can't just sneak into a classroom, I don't think."

"Top Three Hiding Places in Your Home?" Clara continued.

"Replace it with Classroom Number and Time Class Meets," added Dewey.

"Siblings (names and ages)?" Clara posed with doubt.

"No," replied Dewey. "Replace it with 'Best School Friends.'"

"Pets? Parents' Names?"

"Replace with 'Possible Snitches in Class,'" said Dewey, slowly thinking aloud as he suggested it. "And add 'Name, Description, and Subject of Teacher Causing Problem.'"

"'Problem Parent(s) Cause You?'" Clara finished reading the form while still adding, deleting, and revising.

"'Teacher,' of course," Dewey tilted his head to the side, gesturing with both palms up, acknowledging the obvious revision.

"Great!" he added. "Anything else?"

Before they could think more, however, Dewey got a text from his mother reminding him that he needed to watch his little sister, who they called Pooh Bear instead of Emma, in about fifteen minutes.

"You'd better go, sir," cautioned Clara as she did a "save as" of the new document. "I'll get this finished up for tomorrow. You know your mother doesn't like when you're late."

"Come here, Wolfie. Come say 'bye' to me before I go! Come on, Wolfie!" He pranced over and dropped his one-and-only old shabby Skunky in front of Dewey. Dewey certainly wouldn't be the one to break it to him, but it wasn't so one-and-only—Wolfie actually had ten of those skunks, so that one would always be handy to find. He remained none the wiser, as he had no idea that Clara owned ten different Skunkies, or so she and Dewey assumed. Really, who could know such things for certain? Maybe Wolfie loved all ten with equal passion, as a mother dog loves each of her puppies.

"Oh, sorry buddy, I gotta go now. Clara, throw his Skunky, would ya? I feel bad!" Wolfie grabbed the skunk in his own mouth, shook him hard in the air. It always made Dewey laugh when Wolfie thrashed Skunky around like that. He picked up the flat black and white furry friend between his teeth and shook it as hard as he could from side to side, his head moving so fast it looked like he had three heads.

"Go, on, boy! Kill it!" laughed Dewey.

"Okay, okay. Just a few throws," agreed Dewey. That proved challenging though. Wolfie sure might like to have someone throw Skunky to him, but he had a hard time with the "letting go" part. He clenched his teeth down tightly on Skunky's floppy stuffed body.

"Boss," cautioned Clara. "You need to go, and Wolfie needs to see a man about a horse."

Dewey looked confused.

"Oh, you young Snapchatters. He needs to take a wee. And you need to skedaddle."

"Oh! Okay, okay." Dewey laughed. "I'm going." Dewey gave Skunky one big yank out of Wolfie's mouth and lobbed it long and hard across the room for good measure.

"See you tomorrow, Clara."

"Until tomorrow, Dewey Fairchild, Teacher Problem Solver."

Recorder Mrs. Décorder

"Well," Dewey began, feet up on his desk and the form up on his computer screen, "we can see right here that you have a considerable teacher problem with Mrs. Décorder." Dewey then read back to Bryan what he had written under the category of "Problem Teacher Causes You."

"'She's rather unconventional!'"

"Right?!" Bryan nodded, eagerly agreeing with his own words as Dewey quoted them.

Dewey continued, raising one finger pointed at Bryan. "You cope by goofing off. Any sensible kid would do the same. So, I'm going to need to gather more information on her to help," he concluded.

At that, Clara pulled out a thin, black pen from the desk drawer.

Where did Clara come from? Bryan wondered. *Had she been here the whole time, or did she just get here?* Bryan felt unsure, but there she stood now, all four-feet-nine-inches of her. She held in her other hand a plate of warm oatmeal cookies—no raisins, of course. Only a rare breed of kid wanted a shriveled-up, dried-out grape in their baked goods, she had always reasoned. Chocolate chips made a most suitable substitute for raisins.

She handed Dewey the pen and offered Bryan a cookie.

"Oh! Thanks!" replied Bryan.

When Dewey just stared at the pen in his hand, she reached over, pressed down on the pen's clip, and it began to speak:

"'Well, we can see right here that you have a considerable teacher problem with Mrs. Décorder. She's rather unconventional!!'

'Right?!'

'You cope by goofing off. Any sensible kid would do the same. So, I'm going to need to gather more information on her to help.'"

Whoa! A recorder pen! Dewey raised one eyebrow in admiration at Clara. *Where did she get this?* he wondered.

As Bryan chewed on the flat, dense, and delicious cookie, Dewey looked for the "on" switch to try make it record again.

"It's voice activated, sir," explained Clara.

"Testing, testing. One, two, three," Dewey spoke into the pen. He pressed the pen's clip, as Clara had done, triggering it to repeat his words.

"'Testing, testing. One, two, three,'" played back.

"Awesome," approved Dewey.

"Awesome," agreed Bryan.

"Here you go," offered Dewey, handing Bryan the pen with care and ceremony, like it was the key to a trusted kingdom. He lowered his voice. "Bring this espionage equipment with you to class the next couple of days to surveil the subject in her habitat. Then dispatch the data back here this weekend. We'll launch a full-scale operation as soon as we've completed the undercover part of the mission, then we'll review and analyze the evidence. Don't worry, Bryan. We'll safeguard a solution, or my name isn't Dewey Fairchild, Teacher Problem Solver."

Technically, he hadn't earned that title yet—Teacher Problem Solver. But that pen had really upped his game.

Bryan nodded affirmatively and helped himself, with Clara's nod of approval, to another cookie on his way out.

You know, Clara?" Dewey said running his fingers

through his hair, until it got snagged in a small knot. "Maybe I should get one of those fedora hats."

Sliding the plate of cookies over to Dewey, Clara smiled warmly and sat down at her desk to work.

Dewey stacked the cookies, one on top of the other, to make a tower. Thin and neat, each one lined up perfectly, as his thoughts drifted from fedora hats to his homework, and how he didn't feel like doing it. He wondered what else he might find to do first.

Suddenly, while in the perfectly happy place Clara sometimes called woolgathering, Dewey's heart leapt into his throat, and his fingers tingled hot with fear. Clara had let out a bloodcurdling scream.

Dewey had never heard her raise her voice before, let alone scream, so the moment not only alarmed him because it startled him unexpectedly, but also because he suddenly feared for her life. As he moved toward her, he could hear her yelling at someone.

"Oh, I'll tie your tail in a knot. I'll cut off your little ropey tail. Think you can hide from me? I'll slap you asleep, and then I'll slap you awake for sleeping. You hear me? Are you a mouse or a man? Come out here and fight like a man. I'm gonna stomp a mudhole in you and walk it dry. I r—"

Dewey looked into her wide, terror-filled eyes. "What?" he interrupted her. "What is it?!" he implored when she silently shook her head.

"Mouse," she now whispered so softly that he could barely discern her words.

"A mouse?" he repeated, half comprehending what she'd said. "You saw a mouse?"

Clara's eyes got wider, and she nodded. He looked up at her as she stood in the middle of her desk.

He looked around. "Where?"

She pointed to the corner of the room. Dewey walked over, and his heart rate began to settle back down as he acclimated himself better to the situation.

"I don't see it. Wolfie, come here, boy. Look for a mouse, would ya?"

Wolfie slept soundly on the cushion. He looked up when Dewey called him but, evidently, followed the lead of Dewey's heartbeat, and settled back down. Surely, Clara's scream must have startled him too?

"You're sleeping through all of this?" laughed Dewey. "Oh, that's just great," he shook his head in disbelief before addressing his panic-stricken assistant again. "Clara, I don't see it. I'll keep looking. Maybe we have a mouse problem."

"Oh, don't say that, sir. No, I'm not coming here. I won't. I can't."

"Clara, I don't get it. It's a mouse. It's about the size of your thumb."

"I don't care for rodents. I'll be back when it's gone.

Let me know." Then, she folded her arms over her chest and just stared at him waiting patiently.

"Oh. Oh!" replied Dewey, finally catching on as he walked over and motioned her to the edge of the table. She hesitated. He looked down at the ground and all around for her.

"All clear. Come on."

He expected that she would step down. Instead, she nosed her toes out over the desk, took in a small breath, and hopped, landing like a trapeze artist landing into her partner's arms. What a sight they must have made: a ninety-four-year-old Clara in Dewey's spindly eleven-year-old arms. The Flying Cottonwood Extravaganza. He carried her over to the Gator and prepared to set her down, but he could feel her begin to inch up his neck, so he lifted the Gator with them both and, once up top, sent her safely on her way.

She left without so much as an, "I'll see you, Boss".

Wow, thought Dewey. *I've never seen her like this.*

"Wake up, Dog. We've got work to do." He roused Wolfie, and together, Wolfie and Dewey managed to delay starting his homework by spending the next few hours looking for a wayward mouse. Eventually admitting defeat, Dewey decided he'd better return Wolfie to Clara's house, so Dewey could do some homework, and Wolfie could have his dinner. Anyway, he certainly wasn't proving to be a great deterrent or hunter of mice, despite his hunting experience with a two-dimensional, sewn-together, floppy, incredibly-realistic skunk.

Dad's Got Homework

As the sweet taste of summer days slipped away from the students, the school year got up and running for someone else too—Dewey's dad. Dr. Don Fairchild, DDS, had gone back to school to live out his dream—to become a math teacher. Unlike any of Dewey's friends who preferred their summer days spent in camp or free and easy, his dad had gotten a head start on things by choosing to take summer school. When his dad asked if he wanted to join him and take some enrichment classes, Dewey's response was "No thanks, Dad."

This fall Don Fairchild was well on his way to becoming a teacher, student teaching his own class.

Dewey hoped it would soon mean less attention on his own math and more attention on other kids' math instead.

Right now, his dad was holed up in his makeshift office in the backyard guest-house with papers all over his desk. He had three yellow pencils with pink pearl cap erasers sticking out of his brown hair that made him look like a giraffe with knobby horns.

Dewey poked his head in the door to the sight of his dad's messy office space.

"Hey, Dad. How's it going? I'm home. Mom left to run her errands."

"Good. Good," he answered without looking up from his computer screen as he turned the page in his book and patted his desktop, looking for a pencil.

Dewey slid one out from his dad's curly brown head of hair and handed it to him.

"Oh, thanks. I'll be right with you—as soon as I jot down this idea."

After flipping the pages a few times back and forth, he finally scribbled something down and looked up at Dewey.

"How was your day?"

"Eh, you know. The usual."

"Tell me something you learned in school today." Dewey's dad took a small plastic pack of peppermint toothpicks out of his red plaid shirt pocket and offered one to his son before sticking one in the side of his mouth. He'd developed a wee bit of a belly as of late, and he hoped the toothpicks would distract his interest in sweets. He found himself always longing for them due to the mysterious smells of baked goods wafting over from the neighbors'. Dewey's mom had suggested that perhaps some more long walks might be more beneficial than peppermint toothpicks as a regimen, but thus far, this seemed to be his preferred strategy. Dewey shook his head to decline the offer.

"Like what? I don't really remember," he replied honestly. His school day seemed like a long time ago.

"Did anything funny happen today?" He wriggled the toothpick around with his tongue.

"Um, probably. Wait, haha! Yeah. Something did. In P.E. You know how all the lanes at the pool have numbers? Well, Coach B. doesn't want everyone diving in the pool at once, so he had us count off, one to ten so he could send us over in groups of ten to one of the six lanes."

"Okay," Dewey's dad encouraged him to continue.

"So, we go, 'one, two, three, four, five, six, . . .' and Max says 'three' and then everyone yells at him, and we have to start all over counting off to ten. Everyone is freezing cause we're all wet, and the natatorium is like 65 degrees. When we get to 'ten,' Coach sends the group to a numbered lane and the counting starts again. You'd think this would be easy, but it's not because at least three times some ding-dong messes up the counting and Coach has to start that group over. Finally, he's gets all of us at our lanes.

"So, we're all lined up shivering. Coach wants to make sure there are only six of us jumping in the pool at once. He blows his whistle and says, 'Okay! Ones! Jump in!' He figures the number ones from each lane would jump.

"Still following?" checked Dewey.

"I think so. He wanted one kid from each lane to jump in the pool and start to swim, right?"

"Right! And they do, but those bozos from lane one think he means *them* and all ten of them jump into that dinky lane at once!"

"That's crazy!" Dewey's dad replied and his brown eyes crinkled as he smiled.

"I know! Hilarious. Ryan and I just stood there laughing. It was a total traffic jam of elbows and knees hitting each other in lane one! I'm not kidding. There were feet inside of noses and heads underwater. Dad. Literally. There were ten boys on top of one another. Every time one picked up an arm or a leg they hit somebody," Dewey laughed again thinking about it.

"Coach ran over to the edge of the pool, blowing his whistle and yelling. Then he just gave up and started cracking up."

Dewey's dad laughed. "That's pretty good."

"Well, I better go in. I'm supposed to be playing with Pooh in there."

"Okay. I should be done in another thirty minutes or so."

While Dewey played a bit with his little sister Pooh, he thought about Clara and how upset she'd been about the mouse. He'd never seen her upset about anything.

"Hey Pooh-bers, I have some homework and stuff I need to research. You want to come sit on my bed and read or color while I do some work?"

"On your bed?!" Pooh felt gleeful to be permitted on Dewey's bed. He didn't even like her in his room these days.

"Yeah, sure. If you can let me do some work."

"I can do it, Dewey."

Dewey spread a beach towel down on his bed, and she hopped up with a big box of crayons, three coloring books, and a blank pad of paper.

Dewey sat down at the computer and typed in "people who fear mice."

"Dewey. I dropped my crayon," declared Pooh.

Dewey, deep in his reading, did not hear her so she announced it louder.

"Dew-eeey! My crayon fell!"

"Argh," he complained and picked it up for her.

Once back at the computer, Dewey learned they termed it musophobia, and that among phobias, it was pretty common. Still, he didn't know why Clara had it and what should be done about it.

He began to read some more sources and searched on Google Scholar where the articles were a lot more complicated and confusing.

"Dewey. I dropped my crayon," said Pooh.

"What? Again? Pooh. Just leave it. I'll get it later."

"I need the pink one," she objected, her blue eyes begging.

"Pooh," Dewey growled as he got up and handed it to her. "Hold onto them better. I'm busy working, okay?"

"Sure, Dewey!" she sang, going back to her coloring.

No sooner had he sat down to read about frequency, intensity, dura—"Dewey. It dropped."

"Argh! Let's just make this easier!" he went over and dumped the whole box on the carpet.

"Dewey!" Pooh objected.

"Here," he entreated, "move off the towel." And he began to tug it out from under her.

"Hey! My picture," she fretted.

Dewey moved her picture and all the books off the

towel. Then he yanked it out from under her like a magician with a tablecloth full of dinner dishes.

"Down here," he insisted as he spread the towel out on the carpet, kicking and rolling the crayons out of the way.

"Now, just get your crayons as you need them. Seriously, Pooh, I gotta work."

"It's too soft."

He looked around his room for something to make the carpet solid under her paper. Dewey got her a big book. After he set it down, he bared his teeth and mimed as if he were about to bite her head.

Then, he pat her silken chestnut brown hair and said, "O-kay, back to work everyone," and took two steps toward the computer.

"Can we play Candy Land?"

Dewey pivoted on his right heel, took two steps back to her, and gathered up the four corners of the towel up with Pooh Bear and all her stuff inside.

Pooh Bear giggled and laughed as Dewey lugged her down the hallway and dropped her on the couch.

"No," he puffed. "We can't play it. But you can watch it." He turned on the movie, blanketed her legs with the towel, kissed the top of her head, and walked out.

Exam Day

A couple days later, Dewey reassured Clara up and down that he and Wolfie had searched the place, also up and down, and seen neither hide nor hair of that critter. Still Clara wouldn't return.

"I'm sorry, sir. I just can't," she lamented.

Clara had gone through Bryan's recordings at home, though, and edited out the parts that didn't seem of interest or helpful, and she emailed Dewey a clean copy of the "best (and the worst) of" Mrs. Décorder's class.

It turned out Dewey's dad wasn't the only one who used his hair as a pencil case. Bryan also found it convenient to stick pencils there, especially on test days. Since his hair only had soft waves, not the tighter curls of Dewey's dad, though, he had to twist and twirl the pencils around a bit to get them to hold. His hair stuck up, wild thick twisted snakes curling their way around number two pencils.

"Ohh," observed Mrs. Décorder, tilting her head sideways and pausing to look at him. "Now, there's something you don't see every day, Ryanandbryan." When Mrs. Décorder spoke, her words had that gooey quality as if she had a caramel in the back of her throat.

The other kids began to laugh now, noticing how Bryan looked like some sort of screw-horned antelope.

"When I was a girl," she recalled, twirling her fire-red hair in her fingers, "I used to curl my hair like you do, Ryanandbryan. I made bee-yoo-tiful pin curls." She drawled long on the vowels making the word "beautiful" thick and quaggy as she spoke.

Bryan just stared stone-like at her not sure what to say. He had quickly shoved a couple pencils in his hair on his way from his locker to class so as not to have to lug his binder. What was all this talk about hair?

She held the exams in her hands and sat down on her stool. "It's best, of course to start with damp hair. Do you find that as well, Ryanandbryan?"

"Huh?" the pen recorder taped his reply.

"Well, it's easier to work with that way," she told the class. "Next come the sections. Yes, that's right. Is that right, Ryanandbryan? Sections come next, of course, that's right."

Bryan looked at Ryan and slowly slid the pencils out of his hair hoping that might somehow save him from whatever came next. He looked at the clock. She was using up their test time. Maybe they wouldn't have to take the exam!

Mrs. Décorder stood up. "Pinch and roll, pinch and roll. I'd pinch and roll each sectioned strand of hair, and of course bobby pin it close to my head. Oh, Ryanandbryan, you do bring back memories.

"The bobby pin," she continued, "is a fine little scientific invention, is it not?" she asked the class. "Who would like to guess where we get the name?"

The class, only too happy to try to delay the exam attempted a round of guessing the origins of the name bobby pin.

"His son was named Bobby?" asked AJ.

"No. Good guess, though," Mrs. Décorder drawled.

Sadly, though they had no more guesses. The name Bobby meant nothing to them. They didn't know any Bobbys. So the brainstorming stalled.

"For the hair bob!" she sang.

"Who's he?" asked Katie.

"Not who, what! The hair bob of the 1920s. The bobby pin was very useful for that particular hairdo and was invented during that era."

"Ryanandbryan seems to prefer pencils over bobby

pins. I'm sorry we don't have more time to hear about your choice today. Ryanandbryan, you understand, we have an exam to take. Don't you?" He just stared at her.

"I *would* like to hear more about how you twist your hair. I always thought you had to *roll* not twist. Twisting makes for a fuzzy coiffure."

Bryan gave her a big closed mouth smile, and Mrs. Décorder went back to handing out the exams face down. They only had fifteen minutes left to take their tests.

"Roll not twist?" Ryan baited him.

"I have no idea what she's talking about." Bryan whispered back.

"Now, Ryanandbryan, no talking," she drawled. "Go ahead and turn over your tests, class."

Bryan finished his test easily before the bell. There sat Mrs. Décorder at her desk, grading a stack of papers and unaware of how many eyes wandered to others' exams. The projector sat right next to the turn-in basket.

He dropped his test in the basket and stood quietly in front of the room.

These were just the moments that got him into trouble. Bryan felt the sudden temptation to throw an image of Medusa up on the SMART Board with Mrs. Décorder's face. All it would take would be a few clicks, and all those pin-curl snakes would be hers!

Later, Bryan couldn't be sure if it was the bell that saved him, or his own self-control, but he ended up leaving the class. At least for today, no one would be turned to stone.

"Okay," Dewey laid out to Bryan when they met again after he'd had a chance to review the recordings over the weekend.

"Here's what we're going to do: you gotta learn to make nice more. I don't think we're going to make her less, um, eccentric. So you gotta play to her soft spot. Bring her an apple. Clean her SMART Board for her. Make her a lunch. Start making nice!"

"Seriously? I mean, she's not a bad person. It just seems weird, I guess, to be nice to someone who is making you miserable."

"Well, try it out for the week, then come back and let me know how it's going. Don't come on too strong at first. Save the big ones like making her lunch for when you really mess up big," directed Dewey.

"Okay. I'll come sooner if I get stuck. Otherwise, next week." Bryan looked around for any signs of some cookies that might be coming his way. Nothing.

Shoot! Thought Dewey. *I forgot to take cookies out of the freezer!*

"Frozen cookie?" offered Dewey.

"Yeah, why not," nodded Bryan, never one to turn down a cookie of any sort.

Dewey went to the freezer and found a plastic bag with some standby chocolate chip cookies. Clara always thought of everything, even when he did not.

"Here you go," he offered Bryan three to make up for forgetting to defrost them.

"Thanks!" accepted Bryan.

With that, Bryan left with a boost up from the Gator Electric.

"I think we're on to something, Clara," Dewey spoke to the four walls to break the silence after Bryan left. "I think we've got this one! I just gotta figure out how to get you back again," he sighed, and, chewing on a frozen chocolate chip cookie, he sat down at his desk to think.

Food Groups

Dewey loved eating. Dewey did not love to eat everything put in front of him. Squishy things like yogurt or melted cheese made him almost gag. So he didn't like macaroni and cheese or grilled cheese. He liked pizza though. He wasn't a psycho.

He also preferred to eat his food in courses, and he didn't like things mixed together. Peas and pasta and chicken tasted fine, but each had its own spot on the plate. Dewey would eat all of one item, then the next, and finish the last. It used to drive his mother crazy. He knew this because she used to say things like, "Dewey, you're driving me crazy!" Now though, she seemed used to his ways and just glad he ate well from each of the food groups.

Health class was teaching a lot about food groups lately. They had to look at what they were eating at home, paying close attention to the ingredients and how much they ate of each food, then compare it to some government chart. Dewey didn't really care very much about charts. He did, however, care a good deal about snacks, which accounted, in part, for his great love of the vending machines. He thought the whole idea that you could just go and get something you want whenever was groundbreaking! He and his best friends, Colin and Seraphina, met up there whenever they could between classes and during the break.

No one spoke at the vending machines. They just fed their dollars in and waited for it to drop the food. Chips, popcorn, corn nuts, granola bars, overpriced beef jerky, and, on occasion, Tootsie Rolls or M&Ms. You'd never know when those would be there. Pop-Tarts. Great idea, but they had no toaster. Some kids microwaved it during lunch break, but Dewey did not recommend that. Microwaved Pop-Tarts meant a tart without the pop which seemed to defeat the whole point completely.

The extent of the vending machine area conversation usually consisted of "what should I get?" or "can I have a dollar?" Beyond that, kids just grabbed their grub and headed to the main lawn area to hang out.

There they'd sit down, eat their snack, and talk about whatever happened in class.

Today, Colin was fired up because the charger for his mini quad-copter had finally arrived, and now he could fly it again. He had lost his first charger, and the copter died so it had been just sitting on his shelf for months. He liked to fly it around his mom's condo building and sometimes, on the weekends, in the empty tennis court at the nearby school after the security guard left. The charger finally arrived last night, so he had it all charged and ready to go.

"You should come over right after we get out for the weekend. Ask your mom if you can come home with me," Colin said, ripping a piece of beef jerky between his teeth, betraying his dimples.

"How can you eat that stuff?"

"It's good," replied Colin, shoving a piece under Dewey's nose. "Have some."

Separately, each of Colin's soft black curls formed a soft, complete letter "o." Together, they made one big arc of curls, with a few random tendrils that hung down over his forehead and the back of his neck. All those little "o"s had piled atop one another so much over the summer that it was even longer than Dewey's hair.

"No thanks," he declined, pushing away Colin's hand.

"So," continued Colin, tearing off another bite.

"Can you come?"

"Yeah," replied Dewey. "I think that should be fine. I'll ask my dad if I can go home with you. Did you get the extra propellers too?"

The warning bell for class rang so they gathered their things. Each headed off in a different direction, and Dewey never got his answer to the propeller question. He hoped Colin had gotten them because he and Colin always crashed the drone, and those things broke so easily.

"Where the binder reminder is Seraphina?" Dewey wondered aloud, suddenly realizing that she hadn't shown up for a snack with him and Colin during the break.

Science Time

Meanwhile, back at his elementary school, Bryan headed into Mrs. Décorder's class with a beautiful farmer's market honeycrisp apple that he'd swiped from the fridge that morning.

"Hi, Mrs. Décorder. We went to the farmer's market, and I picked out this apple for you." He handed it to her on the palm of his hand like a child offering a horse an apple, hoping it won't bite.

"Oh, why thank you, Ryanandbryan!" replied Mrs. Décorder. When she spoke, she kept her painted red lips together, opening only a very small hole just big enough for the words to escape. "I'll enjoy this with my lunch today very much. Yes. Very much." She took the apple and placed it directly into her paper lunch bag on the corner of her desk.

Bryan smiled and replied. "Sure. Honeycrisp, Mrs. Décorder. They're coming in season now."

"Oh, yes. Yes, they are, aren't they, though?" she agreed through that little round hole of a mouth.

Bryan sat down and tried to focus on something other than how idiotic he must look to the other kids now arriving to class, some of whom surely caught wind of their conversation.

He sat at his desk and busied himself with his backpack when Ryan came in and plopped down next to him. The bell rang just as Ryan sat, and Mrs. Décorder stood up at the SMART Board to put up a quick-write for them to begin class.

He gave Ryan a shrug and looked up at the board.

The prompt read: "What is time?"

Argh. "What is time?" *She knows what time is. I have nothing interesting to say,* he thought, staring at his paper. Time is what's ten hours ahead in Japan. Time is what disturbed his delicious slumber this morning. Time is that big clock on the wall dragging right now.

"So," began Mrs. Décorder after a few minutes had passed, "Who would like to share some of what they wrote?" The hand on the clock clicked to exactly 10:23.

A few hands went up, and Joanna read first. "Time is a very interesting idea. Before the Big Bang, there was no time at all. It's always going nonstop, and yet we can't really see it happening. People and flowers grow old and show us signs though that time is passing, so we know it is real." 10:25. *Time was sure moving slow,* thought Bryan.

"Oh, yes, veeeery nice. Yes, tha-nk you, Jo-a-nna," drawled Mrs. Décorder. "Wh-oo would like to be next? Of course, sunny yellow daffodils are a wonderful sign that spring has arrived. There's the Golden Ducat, the Petit Four, oh! What about the Rip Van Winkle! There's a variety! Oh, trumpeter flower! Hear my call! Time, time in-deed.

"Who else would like to read?" She barely paused long enough to call on someone and went on waving her arms up and down as she spoke. "Sun up. Sun down. Sun up, sun down. Day, night. Oh!" she cater-wauled running across the room grabbing into thin air as if to catch it. "There goes a second! Oh, wait! There goes another one. Shh!" she lowered her voice. "No one talk. Quiet now . . . oh my, a minute has passed never to return!"

Bryan tore out a piece of paper from his binder and his hand scribbled: "TIME: AT EXACTLY 10:32 EVERYONE PICK UP THEIR SCIENCE BOOKS AND DROP THEM ON THEIR DESKS TOGETHER. PASS IT ON!"

He tapped Ryan on the shoulder and off it went. It was 10:28.

"So, who else will read what they've written?"

No one volunteered.

10:29.

"Who else? Will."

"Um, okay," replied Will.

Mrs. Décorder just stared back at him with her red painted lips, her green pants, and her red hair spiked a bit like a rooster's comb, so Will began to read.

"When I think of time—" Will read his story about being late to elementary school two years ago because of construction for a new metro line. Bryan found it about as riveting as flossing his teeth, but he and the whole class sat on edge watching the second hand of the clock move. 10:31.

10:32.

On the dot, the whole room shook like a bomb hit it as every kid—except for poor Will—dropped their science book on their desktop.

A two second pause hung in the air, and then Mrs. Décorder yelled, "DR-OP! COVER!" and dropped to the floor, crawled under the desk, and folded her arms to cover her head.

Silence.

Then came the giggles and a few suppressed chuckles.

After a few moments, Mrs. Décorder came out from under the desk and smoothed her disheveled clothes back into place.

She took out her apple, sat down, and munched on it at her desk. "I think," she muttered, "it's *time* for a break."

Sealing It Up

Dewey determined that he could seal up the entrances to their attic office, and he could prevent mice from entering through the ducts or the kitchen. All the cracks, holes, and openings had to be sealed with cement, metal, or caulk. But most importantly, Clara's cookies and baking ingredients needed to be closed in sturdy containers.

Okay, thought Dewey. *Doable.*

"I need a couple days, Clara. I'm going to make sure the office is 100% sealed up and mouse-proof, so you don't have to worry," Dewey declared to Clara on Facetime.

Clara was touched. She usually handled the office and facilities.

"Thank you, sir," she blushed, though Dewey couldn't see the pink rise to her cheeks because she hadn't turned on her camera. "I don't know why I dislike them so. I always have, though."

"No worries, Clara. I got this," Dewey assured her.

"How are things going with Mr. Frenchie?"

"He's coming by again soon, actually. I have a lot to catch you up on! Can I see Wolfie?"

Clara turned on her camera and picked Wolfie up onto the couch.

"Wolfie? Hey, Buddy!"

Wolfie looked around the room and out the window, totally baffled. He knew the sound of Dewey's voice and kept looking around for him.

He jumped down and waited at the door.

"No, Wolfie. I'm here, on the computer! Come here!"

Wolfie's ears went up at the sound of Dewey's voice, but he quickly got bored and left the room.

"Sorry, sir."

Dewey laughed. "That's okay. But I need to get you guys back here. This is terrible! Oh, I think I hear Bryan coming. I'd better go."

"Okay, Boss."

"We'd better get you back here soon," Dewey repeated.

Bryan recounted all that had occurred, starting with how he'd done his best to befriend Mrs. Décorder, but he had not been overly successful.

"Maybe," suggested Dewey, "we're not going about this the right way. I mean, let's face it. She's definitely a challenge, but you're kind of part of the problem."

Bryan's mouth opened to object, but before he could get the words out, Dewey shoved a chocolate crinkle cookie into it.

Thankfully, Dewey remembered this time to defrost from Clara's still solid supply of frozen cookies. Dewey had no intention of working his way through them all before he got her back.

"So let's just say," Dewey continued, "that Mrs. Décorder, with all her eccentric ways, came to me as a Student Problem Solver and asked me to help her with *you*. I think I'd tell her to fight fire with fire."

Dewey had caught Bryan's interest now. "Go on," he encouraged as he swallowed.

"You're just going to have to help her to help you. Go accept responsibility for what you did, but at the same time, you gotta do something to get kids to think she's more fun and isn't just so . . . I don't know, whatever it is that she is."

"Yeah. Okay. I'll try it, I guess. But how? I don't totally get it."

"Well, it's like this. What if you helped her get the class to at least appreciate her more by, um . . . let me think . . . I know, have her tell you guys to film your-selves dropping your books, and then filter it, say, as a backwards loop."

"I don't get it," Bryan said again.

"Well, it would be funny, but it would be like her way of making you guys 'take it back.' See?"

"Oh. Yeah. I do see. 'Cause it's in reverse. Haha! That's funny. But why, again?"

"You take responsibility for what you did, but you show her how to be more fun about it, so you don't get in trouble, and kids like her better. See?"

"Oh!"

After Bryan headed back out, Dewey walked the perimeter of the office looking for the mouse. He had not been in the attic for a few days, and it felt nice to be back but strangely quiet without Clara and Wolfie.

As he walked along the edge of the walls, he took notes and pictures of any places that looked like they might need sealing up. The attic spanned about 500 square feet, more than enough space for their needs. Medium-tone hardwood covered sound-insulated floors, in addition to a large area rug they'd selected to throw on top, reasoning that it would make sitting on their big floor pillows more comfortable and keep their activity around the office more quiet. They'd selected a shag, ivory carpet that looked like lamb's wool and had a deep, soft thickness underneath their client's fingers and toes.

The walls—also cream—brightened up the space where natural light came in through some long rectangular windows that lined the ceilings above. In the middle of the big room sat Dewey's freestanding desk with his computer, placed so that he faced the large, lime-green pillows where his clients sat. Clara had her own small desk built into the wall, though she rarely sat at it while they worked together. More often, Dewey and his clients would find her in her kitchen alcove baking cookies or standing alongside Dewey and his clients with a plate of cookies.

The main room looked well-sealed to Dewey, but the air conditioning ducts had surely been the issue, he reasoned. Still, he'd go check out the kitchen area first then head up into the air ducts where the clients came in and out.

Clara's kitchen nestled in the corner of the attic, separated from the rest of the room by a sheer panel that allowed the light to pass through. It made not only for a separate space for her to bake, but the panel provided a full-sized screen for them to project images or watch movies on when they had time. Watching movies together was how he and Clara had spent their earliest days when she used to babysit him. These days, though, they would be lucky to slip in even a "Funniest Pets" clip on YouTube. Dewey decided now would be a good time for a little pet levity and loaded one up.

"Let's see," Dewey searched around looking for some Havanese puppies. It didn't matter what they did, they were adorable little fluffballs of fur. Dewey smiled. He loaded another "Funniest Pets" and watched a cat chase a small grey mouse endlessly around a car tire like on a hamster wheel and laughed. "Maybe that's all we need. A cat!" he smiled.

Next came a cat trying to catch a fish on an iPad. "Dumb cat!" *Oh!* thought Dewey. *Keyboard Cat!* He loaded the link and the electronic keyboard began, electronic drum kit and piano merging as that earnest orange marmalade cat in blue scrubs dug into the ivories. It didn't matter how many times he watched that cat, it made him laugh. He knew he should get back to work, but YouTube put as Up Next "Goat Scream Music." Nothing made Dewey and Colin laugh harder than those goats bleating between the verses of the artist belting it out. He couldn't resist.

How he'd gotten so quickly from fluffy Havanese puppy's trying to hop up onto a lawn chair to goats butting into Taylor Swift's musical anthem was any-body's guess, but he needed to get back to Clara and Wolfie, so he turned off the videos and walked around to the other side of the screen.

There was a large, white wooden island in the middle of the partitioned space, with grey and white marble top. Above it, on what looked like a ship's anchor, hung a collection of copper pots and pans. Since almost all Clara did in that kitchen occurred on one or two baking sheets, Dewey figured they mostly served as decoration. She had a small, old-fashioned, white refrigerator and built-in shelves. On the right side was a big porcelain farm sink below a round window. He often wondered how it was that Clara had never been seen in the kitchen from the outside, but then he'd remember her short stature, and didn't give it a second thought. The few times he'd been in the kitchen corner, he'd pulled the blinds down. The kitchen had the same wooden floor as the rest of the space, a white oven, and a big hooded pipe to carry the fumes out.

Dewey took pictures of the flour and sugar bags on the counter that needed to be sealed up in mouse-proof containers but found nothing else amiss. He left Clara's domain and strode back out to the Gator lift to see about the biggest task ahead—sealing up the ducts.

What he discovered, though, wasn't as problematic as he'd feared. They already had a door that had to be opened to get into the ducts, and it turned out to be well sealed. He just needed to make sure it would close by itself in case a client forgot. Leaving cookies along the way in the ducts had been part of their signature service, and Clara reasoned they'd help distract any claustrophobics. Dewey made a note that they needed to rethink this tactic.

Lastly, he needed to walk the outside perimeter of the office (which really was just his home). It hadn't rained in quite some time, and the ground felt hard and dry beneath his feet. October was always one of the hottest months in California. Summer days, often cool with morning mist and overcast skies, gave way to more sunny days come fall, with highs in the 80s and 90s. California children picked out their pumpkins in shorts with swimsuits beneath their clothes. Today, a crisp autumn breeze brushed against Dewey's face, and the air left small goosebumps against his bare arms. Dewey might even need to go grab a sweatshirt. The outer walls were secured and sealed. His parents had seen to that.

At last, his feet ached and he yawned. He'd examined every nook and cranny—covered all his bases. He looked at his phone. Since yesterday, three more DMs had come into the business account that no one had reviewed. He needed to get Clara back.

#takeitback

"Well, Ryanandbryan, you make an interesting suggestion there," Mrs. Décorder said after class, sucking on what Bryan had assumed to be a mint of some sort, but realized it to be her own tongue. "How does one go about accomplishing such an achievement?"

Before Bryan could respond, however, she raised the pencil in her hand and touched the eraser to his nose.

"Better yet," she decided, "who is our Tech-No-Helper tomorrow?" She released his nose from her pencil's reach and craned her neck to look at the board. "Katie. Terrific. Tell her what to do."

Bryan and Katie worked out the details, and the next day Katie had the class take out their phones, and told them to each record themselves dropping their book on their desks and Boomerang it.

Blank looks resulted from the students, many of whom looked to Mrs. Décorder to see if she would object to this cockamamie plan.

"Yes, yes. That's right. Do as Ms. Katie asks, please," concurred their teacher.

The room got loud and filled with laughter as kids dropped and filmed.

Bryan looked over at Mrs. Décorder to cue her.

"Yes, well, the other day, you interrupted the lesson by dropping your books and startled me. You," she paused, "should take it back. So, now we're going to take it back. Please take it back, by . . . Katie? By . . .?"

"Posting your videos, '#takeitback,'" she wrote on the SMART board.

The class stared for a beat, looking incredulous. After a few moments, they began to hit play, watching each other's books fly down and then reverse back up. It was a good laugh, not a laugh at Mrs. Décorder, but a laugh with her; though technically, one might note, she stood before them not laughing.

Dewey had devoted a day after school to sealing things up. Clara wanted to pick out the containers to store the ingredients and cookies. She picked out little plates with dome covers for the cookies in the ducts, and clear glass jars with sealing lids to store the ingredients.

Two days more, and the office officially reopened with Clara back to her usual composed self as if nothing had happened. It would be a while, though, before Dewey got the image and sound out of his head of her coming unglued over the small mouse he'd never even caught a glimpse of.

The smell of sugar and butter wafted up his nose as Dewey slid into the office and landed on the cushions. He could almost take a bite right out of the air and taste the warm sweetness as his mouth started to water.

92° Fahrenheit. That's the temperature it takes butter to melt in the oven and then another 218° later comes that smell. Clara had taught him all this one day last year while she baked, and they discussed one of his client's cases that he'd been working on. The cookies go through something that sounds like the "mallard duck effect" or something, and well, really Dewey couldn't recall all that she'd taught him, only that there existed some explanation for why those cookies, right at this very moment, made his whole head think only of cookies and how to eat that smell.

Wolfie ran up to Dewey, whining his excitement to see him after their separation while swinging a wetly loved toy skunk in his mouth for Dewey to throw.

"Hey, boy! Welcome back!" sang out Dewey as he rubbed Wolfie's haunches.

He tried to grab the skunk out of Wolfie's mouth to give it a toss, but Wolfie wanted to play tug-of-war, and his teeth held on tightly to the skunk's head.

Dewey had cookies on the brain, so he gave Wolfie a rub on the head and pushed himself up off the cushions calling out, "Clara?"

She appeared before answering him, balancing a plate of chocolate chip cookies as she hopped her short self and her tall, steadfast grey bun up onto the corner of his desk. Her legs dangled down like a small child's, but her face held the wisdom of someone who understood that when you trade your expectations for appreciation, comfort comes. Dewey began to feel more settled.

He slipped an entire round cookie into his mouth.

"Catch me up, sir."

"Right," began Dewey, leaning back into his office chair. "You know, Clara, the solution took a while this time. Teacher problems might be trickier than parent problems. Or, it just might be that this is all new to me." *I'm sure all your recent days out didn't help,* he thought. He didn't say it, however, being unsure if she would take it as a compliment or criticism. "Finally, though," he continued, "it came to me—straight out of Bryan's own monkey business."

"Oh?" nodded Clara, her eyes looking straight into Dewey's.

"After Bryan pulled that stunt with the textbooks, the whole class, including him, #tookitback. They were like wizards casting a bunch of spells. He said their Boomerangs were hilarious! Even Mrs. Décorder appreciated them! I think she also appreciated them taking responsibility for their actions—which was the whole point, so Bryan wouldn't land his bottom back in Thais' office again! I'm guessing that won't be her last eccentric moment or his last outburst, but at least they see that they can work together. He may be back, though."

With everyone ignoring him, Wolfie threw his skunk in the air, hoping for a toss back. Dewey went to grab it, but as soon as he did, Wolfie bit down again and growled.

"Let go, you crazy dog!" teased Dewey as he tried to get it. Wolfie dropped the toy, and Dewey jumped to grab it, only to have Wolfie cover the skunk with his paws. "Oh, I see how this is going down."

Dewey slowly crept his fingers sneakily toward the skunk, and then, slowly, surely, carefully, GRABBED it! He threw it across the room, and Wolfie barked before running after it.

"Well, Boss, you must have done something right because I just checked, and we have twenty new

Instagram DMs for teacher problems. This one's boring. This one's giving too much homework. Oh, this one's scaring the kids?! Ha! That's no good, is it, now? No, that won't do at all. Should we shift gears a bit this year, sir? We've enough teacher business to keep you busy through the spring!"

"Sure," agreed Dewey. "Why not?" He scrolled through the messages, reading aloud one from William Sanai. "Class is super boring." Then another one from Charlie. "'Too much homework,' he says. That's a good one."

"Well, I gotta go," he handed Clara back her phone. "I've got a ton of homework to do," he sighed. "I can't even think about all these cases until tomorrow."

"No problem, sir. More tomorrow!" Clara smiled as Dewey gathered his things.

It felt good to know Clara stayed behind back in the office with Wolfie. Dewey had a feeling he would be able to focus better on his homework tonight, and that he was going to get a better night's sleep.

Let's Go Fly a Drone

After school let out for the weekend, Dewey headed over to Colin's place to fly the mini quad-copter. Colin had been asking ever since the new battery arrived. The mini quad-copter was about the size of Colin's palm when rested in his hand. Its small component parts made a solid case for indoor flight, but neither of his parents ever seemed convinced.

"Let's fly her!" called out Dewey.

"Her?" replied Colin. "He, she, it. This fine piece of micro machinery is definitely an 'it'!"

Dewey grabbed his phone from his pocket and searched online.

"Here," he read. "'*She* is also used instead of *it* for things to which feminine gender is conventionally attributed: a ship or boat (especially in colloquial and dialect use), often said of a carriage, a cannon or gun, a tool *or utensil of any kind* AND occasionally of other things.'"

Dewey slowed down his reading on the words, "utensil of any kind," and paused before finishing the rest of the sentence for dramatic effect.

"So says Wikipedia. And I know of no better online authority than that." Dewey rested his case.

"Wikipedia," Colin repeated sarcastically. "Not exactly a huge authority, but I guess it'll do. I'm still not calling my drone a she," Colin laughed. "You're an idiot!"

They gathered up their things and headed down the block to the elementary schoolyard tennis courts. Colin carried the drone like a baby chick in his open hand, and Dewey held the controller. When they arrived, no one seemed to be around.

"Looks like a good time to let *her* fly!" joked Dewey.

"Looks like a good time to—" threatened Colin.

"I'm kidding. I'll stop, I'll stop," Dewey chuckled, patting Colin on the shoulder.

Colin laughed, calling him some choice names again, and they set the mini quad-copter down to launch it in the air.

"Go ahead," offered Colin. "You can go first."

The mini quad-copter hovered well and could get

up high in the air, which explained why Colin's dad got upset when they used it indoors. More often than not, it would bump into the ceilings. Here, though, outdoors, with the sky as their ceiling, their height was limitless.

Dewey pressed the left stick slowly, and the copter began its ascent.

"Wait!" called out Colin, and the drone dropped back down to the ground. "Let's go do it on the field where the ground is softer."

That made more sense. Chances of crashing seemed likely.

Once on the field, Dewey managed to get the drone into a good hover. "Now what?" he asked.

"Now give it to me," replied Colin.

Dewey handed Colin the controller. He pushed the stick diagonally up to the right and suddenly the little drone buzzed through the air and did a circle with a loud noise that sounded like a mosquito on steroids.

"Nice!" admired Dewey. "How'd you do that?"

"Pitch and roll at the same time. Here, I'll show you."

Dewey gave it a try and flew the mini quad-copter straight into the ground.

Colin laughed.

As Dewey bent over to pick it up, Colin made a fake fart sound with his mouth. "Ptttt."

"Donkey," objected Dewey.

"Here," laughed Colin, extending his hand. "Let me have a go at it again."

As Colin took over the controller, Dewey heard the buzz of the quad-copter as it whizzed by his head and took off across the field.

"Whoa, did you see that?!" exclaimed Colin. He had guided the drone into almost a complete figure eight.

"Yeah!" replied Dewey. He wanted Colin to do more. In his own hands, somehow, the little copter just seemed to flip and lose control. In Colin's, it maneuvered around trees, around poles, and did flips.

Colin had just settled the small drone on his palm to show Dewey how to do a smooth lift off when Dewey's pocket vibrated. Seraphina had texted.

Where r you? I have news must tell u in person

"She wants to come meet us at your place," Dewey told Colin.

"Sure," replied Colin.

Dewey looked at the time on his phone.

"Oh, that's not gonna work. It's getting too late. I have to get home soon."

Dewey texted her back.

"I wonder what she wants to tell us?" asked Colin, sending the copter off again into the air. "Why didn't she just tell you what's up?"

"Dunno," answered Dewey.

What Seraphina wanted to share would have to wait until tomorrow.

Bored Work

As Dewey sat in math class the next morning, he thought about his next case. According to his paperwork, William wanted "to hit himself over his head with a large mallet" in his Humanities class because the teacher, Mr. Nisano, was "sooo boring."

What makes a teacher boring or not boring? Dewey wondered. *Was it the subject or the teacher?*

"Dewey," Mr. Jordon called on him to answer question three on the SMART Board. Dewey felt his face flush. He had not heard the question. Luckily, he had done the homework and easily went up to the board and completed the problem.

This meant that another five kids would be asked to do the same, and he'd be free to think some more. He made two columns in his binder: "Boring/Not Boring." He tried to consider the different teachers he had and what qualities made them one way or the other.

"Dewey," Mr. Jordon shot a paper-wad through a big straw that hit him on his shirt. "Kindly give us your undivided attention." Not boring. Mr. Jordon, definitely not boring. He'd have to go back to thinking about this later!

"Sorry! Right. Here! I mean, paying attention. Now." Dewey smiled and refocused on the board.

"Gus, here, was wondering how it is that the answer comes out negative. Care to give it a shot?" asked Mr. Jordon.

Dewey looked at it and looked at his own paper. He got a negative, so he looked back at his own steps on the board and tried to retrace Gus's to see where he might have made an error. "A positive times a negative needs to be a negative?" he asked.

"That's always true, sir. Go up to the board and help us out."

Dewey went up and drew on it with his finger, correcting where Gus had made his mistake. He turned to go back to his seat, but Mr. Jordon stopped him.

"Now Dewey, say: 'Gus, do you understand it now, or do you have any remaining questions?'"

Dewey smiled and repeated, "Gus, do you

understand it now, or do you have any remaining questions?"

"I get it," Gus confirmed, nodding.

"Excellent. Now you can return to your seat, Fairchild."

Dewey went back to his seat just as the bell rang. He quickly packed up his stuff. Study hall came next and he would see Colin and Seraphina, and they'd finally get to hear what she had on her mind.

When he got to the class, Dewey found Colin pestering Seraphina to spill the news.

"Oh, good," she turned around and motioned to him to come over. "Hurry up. Sit down. I waited for you." Just like Dewey, Seraphina's eyes were named for the golden hue of the hazelnut shell. But whereas Dewey's eyes were fair, with a yellow ring of sun around his pupil that tinged toward the sea foam greenish-blues, Seraphina's hazel eyes were rivers of forest greens, rich earth browns, and sky blues, flowing into a ring of deep green around each black pool. Right now, her eyes focused in with intent.

"What's going on?" asked Dewey.

"I'm telling you two, but you can't let this leak. It's big."

"What?" Dewey and Colin pressed.

"I don't exactly know," whispered Seraphina. "But I

heard Shawn talking to his guys and he said, 'The kids are *not* going to like this.'" Shawn worked as the custodian who took care of all the grounds and facilities at school. All the kids loved him. If anyone knew of something going on that kids would or wouldn't like at school, it was Shawn.

"We should jus-th-t as-th-k him," shrugged Colin.

Colin had gotten a new retainer, and all his words came out funny.

Before Dewey could speak, the bell rang, and the teacher started taking roll for study hall. Seraphina shook her head emphatically and mouthed, "No!" Her eyes were dark as she reprimanded him for not listening to her.

"I told you," she whispered. "You can't tell anyone. He didn't know I was listening!"

"Okay, okay," Colin nodded back.

They pulled out their work but none of them could focus. What change could possibly be happening that they wouldn't like?

Colin and Dewey whispered and passed notes asking Seraphina to talk more about it, but she tucked their notes away and didn't even look at them for the rest of class.

Dewey turned his thoughts back to William, and he took out his boring/not boring list. He soon got incredibly bored by his own list though. It just seemed so obvious. The boring teachers, well, uh, were BORING. Did he really have to bore himself with why?

His math teacher made them laugh but got them learning at the same time. His English teacher almost never made him laugh, but she totally made the stories they discussed exciting by making them seem real with how she read or interesting with the crazy stuff she had them do. He could tell his science teacher last year cared about science a lot by how excited he got. This year, not so much. *Oh, the boring ones sure do talk a lot,* thought Dewey.

Dewey sat there tapping the point of his pencil in the boring column, trying to think how he might help William's teacher to not be such a bore. *Can you make someone funny or force them to make a subject interesting?* he wondered.

Maybe if he held up cue cards for her, he considered. Or was it a him? He couldn't remember who William had for Humanities. That solution seemed unlikely, but he smiled at the thought of it. Too bad teachers probably wouldn't go for it. Little electronic teleprompters. Haha! The thought of that made Dewey laugh quietly to himself, two almost indiscernible short, fast blasts of air out of his nostrils.

Dewey recalled his own times trapped in classes

with boring teachers droning on and on. The more he thought about it, the more furious he became. They take a bunch of kids who come bounding in perfectly happy and eager, close the door, and wham! Boredom and no escape. In the name of humanity, Dewey would figure out how to right this wrong.

T-issue

Going to the bathroom at middle school was about as enjoyable as going to the dentist. Dewey should know. His dad used to be a dentist, and they had talked a lot about dental visits while Dewey was growing up. He knew just how enjoyable people found them. Plenty of days, Dewey's dad came home with a finger that had bite marks to show for it.

That's probably part of the reason Dewey's dad wanted to be a math teacher—for some crazy reason, Dewey's dad thought kids would like to go to math class more than the dentist. That made Dewey laugh. Although he loved going to Mr. Jordon's class, and that was math, so anything was possible.

Middle school bathrooms had the great time-saving

invention, urinals. They recently installed waterless, no-flush urinals, which generally inspired Dewey to hold his breath. In the final estimation, though, the bathrooms in middle school enjoyed a marked improvement over the elementary school ones, where the little kids kept missing the bowl and left a puddle of pee on the floor.

What he really didn't love, and he'd do his very best to avoid if humanly possible, was going number two at school. He remembered going home one day saying he had a stomachache rather than facing that in elementary school. He was older now, though, and could—if he *had* to—do it. Colin, on the other hand, seemed to have no problem with it at all. In fact, he'd walk right into a stall with his independent reading book and settle in for a "sit-down," as he'd call it, pretty much daily. Dewey tried never to touch Colin's books for that reason.

He and Dewey went into the bathroom at the end of break, and Colin had his book tucked under his arm. Dewey was washing his hands when Colin called out from the stall.

"What? What is this?!"

"What?" asked Dewey through the stall.

"The toilet paper. They changed the toilet paper."

"What do you mean?"

"I don't know. It won't roll! Every time I try to roll it, only one little piece will come off at a time. Check the other stall."

Dewey walked into the other stall and sure enough, the toilet paper roller had been rigged to no longer roll. You could only roll one little perforated piece at a time.

"Same here," reported Dewey. "It's the same paper, I think, but the roller's different."

"That's ridiculous," complained Colin. "How am I supposed to get out of here on time? It's going to take me ten minutes to get enough paper!"

Dewey laughed. The bell rang.

"Come on, Colin. Let's go."

"I can't!" objected Colin. "I'm not ready!"

Dewey laughed again.

"Here, take my book," urged Colin, handing the book under the door to Dewey.

"Uh, no. That's okay. You hold onto it," insisted Dewey.

"I need two hands!"

"Nooo," Dewey reiterated.

Colin growled and stuffed the book under his armpit. Somehow Colin managed and came out, washed his hands, and they ran to their respective classes where they both arrived tardy.

At lunch, Seraphina finally wanted to share more of what she may or may not have heard Shawn talking about, and how this may or may not ruin their first year of middle school.

Colin, however, hardly let her get a word in because he now had detention due to the "toilet paper caper," as he called it.

Dewey's teacher hadn't marked him tardy. She was still getting settled when he slipped in and she hadn't noticed. Colin did not find himself as fortunate, and as a repeat offender, he was being held accountable.

"Wait. I don't get it," asked Seraphina, confused. "You're upset about the toilet paper in the bathrooms?"

"No," explained Dewey. "It's that little dispensing mechanism that has him upset."

"They won't let you get more than one piece at a time."

"That can't be right," Seraphina said doubtfully. "Let me go check." She ran off to the girl's bathroom to see if there had been any changes made there.

"Come with me to the vending machines, would ya?" Dewey asked Colin. Dewey hated going there by himself. Something about it just felt lonely. He loved going with a friend, though, almost more than anything else he could think of at school.

Principal Mayoral restricted when middle school-ers could use the vending machines. Students weren't allowed to use them during the passing periods, for example. But before school, breaks, lunch, and after school, they awaited them in all their magnificence.

Dewey had read that paper items like postcards and stamps first filled vending machines in the 1800s. One great visionary in the late 1800s had stuck gum in there. Tutti-frutti for a penny! In the 1950s, vending machines lined airports selling life insurance policies in case you died on a plane. "Seriously? Who'd even get on a plane with vending machines dispensing those kinds of treats?" Dewey said.

Of course, in Dewey's mind, the drinks and the snacks eventually made vending machines the great invention that they are today. The 1920s had the first drinks dispensed in a cup, and the 1930s had the first bottled soda. At first, it was only Pepsi or Coke, Dewey had read.

Dewey's school permitted no sodas in their vending machines at all. He and his friends had other sweetened drinks and bubbly or regular water, though, which tasted deliciously cold on a hot day.

Today was definitely a chocolate snack bar day. The crowd had died down, and Dewey carefully smoothed and fed his dollar into one of the machines.

"How come we don't have those Smart Machines yet?" Colin asked. "This is so old-school."

"I like putting the dollar in," disagreed Dewey. "You

gotta get it just right." As he said so, his dollar came back out, rejected with the machine's warm hum.

Colin laughed. "Haha!"

Dewey turned the dollar the other direction and tried again. This time the machine grabbed it.

"There you guys are," burst Seraphina, out of breath. "It's true! I can't believe it. You guys have nothing over us girls! We use toilet paper more than you do! That's crazy. Someone has to figure out why they did that."

Dewey's chocolate snack bar plunked down, and the machine dropped back a quarter as change. He shoved the quarter in his pocket, and after quickly removing the wrapper, shoved half of the delicious square brown bar into his mouth.

"Do you think that what they were talking about was the toilet paper?" asked Dewey around a mouthful of chocolate.

"You mean Shawn?" replied Seraphina.

Colin tried to take the other half of Dewey's chocolate bar, but Dewey pushed his hand away.

"Yeah," said Dewey to Seraphina before he snapped a "No!" to Colin, like he was a bad puppy.

Colin whined. Dewey broke him off half of his remaining half.

"Maybe," replied Seraphina. "It's a big pain in the butt, that's for sure."

Colin and Dewey both laughed.

Seraphina then got her own unintended joke and joined in laughing as well.

"I'm not sure, though. Seems kind of silly. Like we'd all be so upset about toilet paper? I don't know . . ."

"Well, I'm upset, alright," complained Colin. "In fact, I'm going to take this to the student body. Who better than the body of the students to deal with an issue that affects the student's actual body. Yes," continued Colin, getting more passionate, "—it's a student issue. It's a tissue issue! It's a T-ISSUE! Quick, Seraphina! This is your kind of thing. Make posters. Make a banner. Do that thing you do!"

"Haha!" Seraphina and Dewey both laughed hysterically at this point at Colin's tissue issue, labeled a t-issue, and just how passionate he had suddenly become about it.

"My kind of thing?" replied Seraphina, winding down her laughter. "I'm a rock collector, not a protester."

"No, but didn't you and Dewey make signs for Peewee when you found him?"

"That's true," chimed in Dewey.

"Oh, well, signs, sure. I can do signs. You want tissue issue signs? Or do you want a campaign?"

"I don't know. I don't know! I just know I can't be

expected to eat lunch, visit the facilities, and get to class on time if I have to partition my toilet paper one piece at a time as I clear the deck!"

Dewey and Seraphina laughed.

"Okay, okay," she reassured. "Let me give it some thought. But we have bigger *issues*, I tell you. We need to figure out what Shawn was talking about before we get any more surprises."

The bell soon rang, and off to class they all went. Dewey stopped at the water fountain before going back to class. He had so many different things on his mind. He needed to sit down and focus on all of this after school today and sort it all out.

Clapper Catcher

That night at dinner, Dewey spoke with his parents about some of the things on his mind. At least he tried to do so.

"Tell us about your day, Pooh."

"I was in the 'Clapper Catcher' group. I called it the Clapper Catcher. The Clapper Catcher is the big machine that takes trash to the dump. See, see, see," she gestured with her little hands as she tried to explain, "the trash truck has a special conveyor belt that has a special shaking mechanism to sort *all* the paper."

Pooh Bear, as the family still called her more often than her given name, used to have a speech problem with her Rs, so she'd have pronounced something more like, "Clappoh Catchoh" last year. But she'd been working on it a lot over the summer, and now she spoke pretty well. *The problem,* thought Dewey, *is she never shuts up.*

"Yeah, that's great," interrupted Dewey. "Listen. Mom, I think som—"

"We found a green bin we want to use for the truck, and next time, 'cause we don't get to meet tomorrow because the Clapper Catchers are going to be in a cooking group. That's gonna be fun because I like to cook. I hope we get to make cookies! Last time, they said we might not get to 'cause Heather is glue-free, and she couldn't eat them."

"I think you mean gluten-free," explained Dad. "That means she can't eat certain kind of flours and wheat and things."

Pooh Bear laughed. "Oh, Daddy! You're funny! Nobody eats flowers! Mommy, Daddy thinks glue-free people can't eat flowers!"

Both of Dewey's parents laughed now as Pooh fed herself penne pasta one tube at a time like coins into a slot machine. Her sparking blue eyes, the only blue ones in the family, served as a reminder of genetics as another kind of slot machine. It was funny how Dewey's eyes looked more like theirs than Pooh's.

Dewey exhaled a short hard breath and served himself some more rice. Even with his older sister,

Stephanie, out at a friend's house for dinner, he still couldn't seem to get a word in edgewise.

That's a funny expression. What did it mean to get a word in edgewise? he wondered as Pooh continued. Dewey pictured a whole bunch of words spilling out all over the place, filling up the air space. More and more and more words tumbled out, getting more and more crowded—and as Dewey tried to get his own words in there, he would have to turn them over sideways, on their *edge* and slip his words in between all of hers.

"Dad. Dad? I wanted to ask you something."

"Yes, Dewey. Yes. Tell us about *your* day," his mother encouraged.

"Oh, my day. I don't know. It was okay, I guess. But when you're teaching your math class, how do you make sure the kids aren't bored?"

Dewey's dad laughed. He'd just started his student teaching at the middle school across town this fall. One of the most enjoyable aspects for him so far was how other people's kids seemed to love the things that his own kids rolled their eyes about at home.

"Well, I sing a little, dance a little. You know . . ."

"That sounds about right," laughed Dewey's mom.

"In *math* class?!" exclaimed Dewey, his eyes opening wide along with a mouth full of dinner.

"Sure! Sometimes random things just happen. I have

that microphone there, and some kid will be funny with it, and then we riff on that for a few minutes as they are settling in. It works."

"Hmm," replied Dewey. He closed his mouth and began chewing again, trying to picture that scene and then trying equally hard not to picture it.

"Sometimes, I tell them a little story about myself, right in the middle of what we're doing. They like that. Or I'll start off class telling them something they think is totally off topic and before they know it, I've slipped math right in under their noses."

Hearing about his dad teaching, simultaneously made Dewey feel kind of proud and mortified.

"We found a green bin that we could use for the truck. Next time we meet we're gonna fill it with water and trash and . . ."

Pooh Bear's words began to fill the air again, but this time, Dewey's thoughts turned back inside his own head to William's teacher problem. He needed to figure out how to help Mr. Nisano not make his students want to head for the hills running.

"Dewey? The salt, please?" his mother seemed to have been asking him already, and he'd missed it.

"Oh, sorry!" he replied, picking up the small round snow globe with the snow white polar bear. The pepper shaker was a matching snow globe with a black bear inside. When Dewey was little, they'd had to put the globes away on a top shelf because he would snow salt and pepper all over the house and their food. Pooh Bear, however, seemed much more "mature" when it came to the salt-and-pepper snow globes, and they'd been able to put them back on the table again.

Dewey, on the other hand, still couldn't stop himself. He salted the table a bit as he passed it over to his mom.

"Dewey," his mom admonished.

"Sorry!" Dewey flashed her a smile and wiped the salt off the table into his hand.

He took the salt and sprinkled it on Pooh's plate.

"Mommy!" she objected loudly.

"Dewey!" This time his mother seemed to be losing patience with him.

"She's done eating," Dewey defended himself and gave Pooh Bear the stink eye for telling on him.

"Nonetheless," his dad chimed in.

"Sorry, Pooh," Dewey uttered remotely.

He felt annoyed with everyone right now. It was just a little salt. He asked if he could be excused and cleared his place. It was Stephanie's night to help do the dishes, but she wasn't here, so he'd probably get stuck doing it.

"Do I have to stay and do dishes? I'm super tired and have some work to still do," he submitted for consideration.

"Go ahead," his mom patted him on the hand and motioned with her chin for him to be excused.

That tight knot of annoyance in his stomach loosened. "Thanks, Mom."

"Yup," she said.

Dewey went up to his room and plopped down on his bed. Here, his thoughts could finally stretch out like his legs and move around more freely.

For better or for worse, Dewey's dad was just being himself in the classroom and that probably made it more engaging. So, what was he supposed to do if Mr. Nisano was just, well, being himself? And himself was just about as exciting as waiting to skip the ad before your YouTube video starts?

This wasn't coming together yet. He got his homework done and washed up. It was getting late, and Dewey really did feel tired. He rolled over and turned off his light to go to sleep just as his dad came in, smoothed his hair off his forehead, and gave him a quick kiss on the cheek.

"Night, Dewey."

"G'night, Dad."

He rolled over and fell quickly off to sleep.

T-issue Redux

Dewey pressed the round, shiny, black button that dropped his bag of smoked almonds with a thud. He grabbed them from the long slot at the bottom of the vending machine and stood, mid-conversation with Seraphina.

"I know!" he continued. "They have bread, fishing bait, sushi, ramen, grilled meat sauce, oh, and I found one with umbrellas!" Dewey had been reading more about vending machines, this time in Japan.

Before Seraphina could react, Colin bounded onto the scene eager to share his own online research.

"Okay, okay, okay! Listen to *this*! I've been looking into toilet paper. You guys just talking about Japan? Did you know some guy there wrote his whole book on an actual roll of toilet paper?"

"Really?" Dewey was surprised to see Colin as he hadn't seen him walk up.

"Yes, and there's so much more! Guess what they used before they had toilet paper?"

"Um, I don't know, rocks?" joked Dewey, crunching on some almonds for dramatic effect.

"Dewey Fairchild! For the love of all that is good and decent!" Dewey laughed as Seraphina gave him a shove on the arm.

"Not so far off!" replied Colin excitedly as he walked them over toward the lawn where they could sit down and talk. "Newspapers, corncobs!"

"Corncobs!" laughed Dewey, his eyes getting wide.

"Did you know right now," Colin plunged on, "most of the world doesn't even use it? Water! That's the universal t.p. Yup, water."

"What's your point?" Seraphina asked as they sat down. "You live among the lucky minority who gets to have a clean *and* dry bottom?" She placed her open hand down on the grass. "Speaking of dry bottoms, is the ground damp?"

"Feels dry," Dewey said, stretching out his legs. "I wonder if they have toilet paper vending machines in Japan? Nah," he went on. "I think they have those cool toilets that wash and dry you and shine your shoes while they're at it."

"A few more pieces at a time is what our cause is about."

"Who's '*our*'?" Seraphina asked.

"Exactly what cause is that, again?"

The bell rang.

"'Who's our?' 'What cause?'" Colin repeated back. "You guys and me. The t-issue. You know, our big issue?"

"Oh boy."

"Oh brother."

They went off to class with Colin yammering on about figuring out the next steps in the plan.

Mr. Hollywood

When his dad picked him up after school, they had to stop at the grocery store. Dewey almost weighed enough now to sit in the front seat, but not quite, so he threw his bag in the front and climbed in back.

"Hey, Dad."

"Hey, Dew."

Dewey always went straight for his phone at that point, but his parents had a no-electronics rule in the car, unless it was a long car trip or traffic got particularly horrible. Still, it was always worth a shot. Sometimes it took them a while to notice.

"Hand it up, mister," insisted his dad.

"I'll put it away," replied Dewey, grinning.

His dad turned on the radio and the game began. Some

oldies song played that he would ask Dewey to identify.

"Um, the Beatles?" He always threw them out as his first guess. "Bob Dylan? Rolling Stones?"

"Dewey, Dewey! Don't just guess wildly. Listen to the sound. They don't all sound alike."

"That's what you think!"

Then, his dad turned the volume up and began to sing. "Tom Petty, man. Tom Petty." Down rolled the window, and down Dewey slid in his seat and tried to disappear into the upholstery of the car.

Seriously, this was torture. He'd rather be home emptying the dishwasher or something.

They got to the store and didn't have many items on their list so they stuck together. As they passed by the toilet paper aisle, it reminded Dewey about Colin, and he told his dad all about his new cause.

"Now that's a cause I could really get behind," chuckled Dewey's dad. "Get it?! 'Get *behind*?'"

"Yeah, yeah, I got it," Dewey smiled at his dad's pun.

When they got to the produce department to get the avocados, Dewey's dad greeted a tall kid with full lips and sleek dark hair whom Dewey didn't recognize. The kid promptly turned about ten shades redder than the tomatoes.

"Hi, Mr. Fairchild. Er, hi. I mean—hi. What are you doing here?"

"Hi, Gabe. Shopping for a few items we forgot the other day. This is my son, Dewey. Dewey, this is Gabe. Gabe's in my math class."

Gabe began to turn around one of the oranges in the display with his fingertips. It slipped out of place, and then so did about eight others, which fell to the floor.

"Oh, shoot. Oops. I got that," fumbled Gabe, picking up the oranges and attempting to stack them without knocking more down. Dewey's dad helped him out.

"Well, see you tomorrow, Gabe. We're making guacamole tonight. I'll let you know how it turns out."

"Oh, yeah. Sure. Bye. See ya. My mom's here somewhere. Okay. Yeah."

"Geez," Dewey laughed when they got out of earshot. "What a dope."

"Aw. What a sweet kid," smiled Dewey's dad. "He's not like that in class at all. Must have thrown him, seeing me in the store like that. Say, Dewey, I think your old dad is becoming some sort of celebrity."

Dewey rolled his eyes.

They walked along and put a few more items in the cart.

"Say, Justin Bieber. Can I get a pack of toilet paper for Colin? Just for fun?"

Dewey's Family
is on a Roll

After dinner that night, Dewey's mom picked up the package of toilet paper from the counter and went to put it away under the bathroom sink.

"Hey, Mom. That's mine. Dad bought it for me to give to Colin."

Dewey explained to his mom all about the t-issue at school and how Colin was all riled up about it.

"Oh, I love a good cause," she cheered. "Let's write him a note of support on one of the rolls of toilet paper!"

Dewey laughed. "That's hilarious! Colin just told me about some Japanese author who wrote a whole book that way."

"I wanna help. Can I help?"

"Sure," Dewey told Pooh. "Why not?" Toilet paper, it didn't seem to him, would stretch her out of her area of expertise too much.

Dewey's mom cleared the table of all the books, dishes, and sweatshirts. Their table got loaded with stuff throughout the week, which meant his mom had both arms full of items tucked under her chin as she walked toward the stairs. "Go get a few different kinds of pens. We want to figure out which one writes best on the toilet paper without leaking or tearing."

"Okay," replied Dewey, staring at his mom turned foreman.

"Pooh B, you make sure the table is all dry," she motioned.

"This is going to be interesting." Stephanie glanced up to contribute that observation from the couch, where she was laying, then returned to her homework.

Dewey's dad was parked in the garage office doing his own homework and lesson planning.

"Okay, Dews, how should we start?" His mom didn't wait for an answer though and just unrolled the paper and began writing:

"'Dear Colin,

We heard that you might have a sticky situation on your—'"

"Mom! NO!" Dewey and Pooh Bear laughed, and Stephanie looked up from her work with her mouth dropped open.

"What? No good?"

"No good!" asserted Dewey more firmly.

"Fine then," conceded Dewey's mom. "You start."

"How about:

'Dear Colin,'"

Dewey's mind was blank.

"'Dear Colin' . . ."

"We hear you have been called to duty?" his mom gingerly submitted.

"Not bad!" laughed Dewey.

"How is that *any* better than Mom's first sentence?" groaned Stephanie.

"No, no. It's more subtle," said Dewey's mom.

Stephanie added only, "Hmm."

"'Dear Colin,'"

his mom continued writing.

"'Your tissue issue,'

no, wait—" She tore off the sheet of toilet paper, squished up what she'd written and started over.

"'Dear Colin,

Your t-issue is a call to duty!'"

"How's that?" She looked up to Dewey, Pooh, and Stephanie for approval.

"Good!" nodded Dewey.

Pooh Bear agreed. Stephanie didn't look up from her book.

"Okay then." She handed Dewey the pen. "You want to write now?"

"No, you print nicer. You do it."

So, they began again, and then it just began to, well, roll out of them.

Somewhere between "flushing with joy," and "ultra-strong-mega man" Stephanie couldn't help herself and began to contribute to the project. By the time they completed it, they were all laughing so hard that they were crying.

"Dewey, hand me one of those other rolls," his mom pleaded so she could wipe the tears of laughter that now streamed down her cheeks—so much you'd think she'd been cutting onions.

When Dewey's dad came in and read it, he laughed at almost every line.

Dear Colin,

Your t-issue is a call to duty! We hope this gift will make you flush with joy!

You are the ultra-strong-mega man who, number one, is going to wipe the administration's t-issue clean and, number two, get the kid who runs back to class there on time! A clip isn't going to make you the butt of anyone's joke! You're on fire! Stop, drop, and roll! Well, we really gotta go now.

Love,
The Fairchilds

"Boy, you guys really were on a roll!"

"Har, har!" replied Dewey, feeling proud that they'd impressed his dad with their humor. This was usually the kind of thing they'd do with his help.

"I helped roll it back up," said Dewey's little sister.

"Good work, Tiger." Dewey's dad pat her head. "I think you'd better go get ready for bed now."

Stephanie, who never had to be told to wash up and get ready for bed because she loved to get into bed and read, had already disappeared for the night. She had been the one to contribute the last line, "we really gotta go."

It felt quietly delightful to Dewey to have Stephanie contribute and be a part of it. He loved when she joined in with them.

"You too, Dews," directed his mom. Dewey gathered up the rolls and put them on top of his backpack so he'd be sure to remember them in the morning. He headed upstairs to bed for the night.

"I'll be up in a few minutes to tuck you in," she said.

When she entered his room, she turned off his light and sat at the edge of his bed. The decals of the planets and stars on his ceiling glowed in the dark overhead.

Dewey told his mom how funny it had been that his dad's student, that Gabe kid, got so nervous in the produce aisle of the grocery store. "He acted like dad was some sort of rock star or something. I'm not even exaggerating."

Mom laughed. "Well, that's sort of sweet," she smiled.

"I guess so. Rock star! Ha! He's just a guy who sings annoyingly loud in the morning and wears bad socks!"

"You don't like his socks?" she laughed. "I had no idea you even noticed."

"They're hard to miss with Big Bird, Darth Vader, and Minecraft Steve on them," he groaned.

Mom laughed again.

"I'll bet his student—what was his name again?"

"Gabe."

"I'll bet Gabe doesn't picture him as a dad with bad socks singing loudly in your kitchen. Can you picture your teachers at home being regular people brushing their teeth and tucking their kids into bed?" she said as she pulled the covers around him. "Probably not," she added and punctuated it with a kiss on his cheek.

"Night, Dews," she walked out and closed his door.

Dewey never even thought about his teachers outside of school. Why would he? But he didn't think he'd be as goofy and nervous as Gabe if he ran into one squeezing avocados, either. Dewey stared up at the ceiling and wondered what his teachers were really like. *Did Mr. Jordan go to the beach? Did Mrs. Harrington eat cereal for breakfast? Did Mr. Nisano wear Captain America boxers and sing in the shower?* Dewey chuckled at the thought.

Then, as if one of those stars on his ceiling shot across the sky, Dewey felt a thought shoot right across his belly. He sat straight up in his bed. Was it possible that Mr. Nisano bored the daylight out of his students, but wasn't a boring person? *Let's face it,* thought Dewey, *if William ran into Mr. Nisano squeezing produce, he wouldn't really know any more about Mr. Nisano than that kid Gabe knew about Dad.*

Dewey could always feel it when he finally began to unravel a knot in a case, and he knew at last he had loosened this one.

He'd go research Mr. Nisano, the home man, not the teacher. Dewey felt certain that once there, he'd somehow find the solution to the problem.

With that, he let out a big breath of air he hadn't even realized he was holding in, settled back down into his pillows, and closed his eyes.

I gotta get rid of these glow in the dark decals one of these days, he thought as he began to drift off to sleep. *They keep me up at night.*

Indispensables

"Look what Dewey gave me!" grinned Colin, and he held up the messaged toilet paper roll.

Seraphina looked right at the roll but hardly noticed it. "I know what's going on. I'm telling you two, but you can't let this leak."

Dewey thought her word choice pretty funny given that they were holding a roll of toilet paper, but he figured this was not a great moment to say so.

"Haha! 'Can't let this leak.' Get it?" Evidently, his mouth worked faster than the filter in his brain.

"Dewey! I'm serious. This is big, and we need to figure out what to do—immediately."

"What?" Colin pressed.

"They're getting rid of the vending machines,"

Seraphina announced in a whisper.

"What?!" cried Dewey.

"No, they're not!" exclaimed Colin. "Why would they do that?"

"I don't know," shrugged Seraphina. "But I heard Shawn talking to his guys about moving them out."

"Well," replied Dewey, already imagining what a bleak and tragic world middle school would be without vending machines. "Now we know what 'the kids will be upset' means. This is beyond catastrophic."

"I know. I knew you'd be devastated. We have to figure out how to put a stop to this—and fast."

"Hey, let's not forget about the t-issue," reminded Colin.

"For crying out loud, Colin!" wailed Dewey. "How can you even begin to compare a piece of toilet paper to a pack of pretzels?! We're talking about indispensables! You're on the level of luxury items."

"*Luxury?* Since when did having enough toilet paper become a perk?"

"Since they're taking away my Funyuns!"

"Okay, you two! We want both, don't we? Stop it. What's the matter with you? Let's figure out how to talk to Shawn, and we can keep working on the t-issue. Don't be so foolish."

"Take away a man's vending machines, and he gets

prehistoric, I'll tell you that much," grumbled Dewey.

"Take away a man's royal paper and he gets pretty cave man too!" chuckled Colin.

"Royal paper?!" laughed Dewey.

"You know you're both nuts!" but she still laughed as well. "Well, what's next?"

The first bell rang.

"UUGH!" they all cried.

"Okay, we'll meet after school to discuss?" asked Seraphina, walking backward toward class.

"I gotta work on a case," Dewey called back. "Tomorrow?" This delay would cause Dewey some anxiety, but he could see no way around it.

Colin just stood there not moving.

"Colin? Class?" called Seraphina. But as the quad emptied out, Colin just stood there.

Wooden Trains

Dewey didn't have time to think about vending machines right now. He stood knee-deep in the logistics of the Mr. Nisano case, figuring out the plans to observe him in his non-school environment. This observation required some undercover work. Mr. Nisano and his home wouldn't be as easily accessible to Dewey as problem parents were during a case. With parents, he always had someone on the inside to let him into the house and show him the best places to hide and observe.

Teachers like Mrs. Décorder might be dull at times, but at least their eccentricities helped distract the students. This case, it seemed, presented an entirely different kind of challenge, and solving it proved more difficult.

"Honest, Dewey. If you gave me a two-by-four, I'd smack myself in the head with it over and over just to break up the time in there," Will had moaned during their interview.

The first step of Dewey's plan was for Clara to fetch him after school so they could follow Mr. Nisano and gather as much intel as possible. Dewey had never been a student of Mr. Nisano, which would make spying easier. If this case had come from the elementary school, where all the teachers knew every kid by sight, Dewey didn't know what he'd have done.

One case at a time, breathed Dewey.

As planned, Clara met Dewey at the pick-up circle. Even though Dewey had outgrown needing a babysitter, Dewey's parents still listed Clara on school paperwork as an approved adult to pick up and care for the Fairchild children. This setup often came in helpful during his cases.

"Clara! Hi," Dewey greeted as he climbed in the back and tossed his bag over the front seat. "We need to go park off-campus and wait for him to leave. I have no idea how long that's going to take. I hope it's not too long."

Wolfie, who had been sleeping in the back, woke up and excitedly licked Dewey.

"Hey, boy!"

Clara pulled around the corner where they waited under a shady tree, eating Butterfinger cookies and talking about what they should do next.

"Well, Boss," noted Clara, "this is new territory for us. Perhaps we just let it unfold and see where it takes us."

That strategy made Dewey a little anxious. He liked to know what he was doing before it happened. But he really didn't have much choice in this case.

Then, it finally happened. After about two pages of begrudgingly completed math homework, one tree pee for Wolfie, and ten cookies, Mr. Nisano exited the school carrying a thermos in one hand, a stack of papers in another, and a messenger bag slung over his shoulder. Clara and Dewey watched him as he got into his car and drove past them.

"Thar he goes." Clara started the engine.

"Oh. Oh! Go, Clara, Go! Follow him!" exclaimed Dewey, totally unnecessarily as Clara, who already had the gas pedal to the floor, hotly pursued their subject like a hound chasing a mechanical hare on a track.

None of this haste proved necessary, and they easily caught up to Mr. Nisano, who wasn't exactly a speedster.

He pulled into the supermarket. With his arms now free of all his teacher gear, he swung them by his sides. His pace picked up a bit while he walked toward the market. The tips of his long fingers reached past the halfway mark of his upper thighs, and each stride, though not rushed, would be about five for Pooh Bear to take to keep up, Dewey estimated.

"What is it about teachers and supermarkets?" marveled Dewey. "Okay, stay here. I'm going in."

Dewey waited for sufficient distance to grow between him and his target before he entered the market to find Mr. Nisano shopping which, given Mr. Nisano's long strides, didn't take long.

Well, thought Dewey sarcastically, *this is going to be an epic adventure.*

Tomatoes. Bananas. Crackers. Cheddar cheese. Half and half. Dewey used his phone to take notes on the items Mr. Nisano put into his cart.

He shops. He eats.

Dewey recorded it all but slowly felt more and more confident that this information was getting him nowhere. He waited, again, while Mr. Nisano paid. He returned to Clara, and they followed the subject to the next stop, which all leading indicators suggested was the teacher's home.

Mr. Nisano entered the house, leaving Dewey and Clara in their car contemplating what to do next. It felt risky to just go peek in his window. What if someone saw him? They decided to approach it more as a stakeout than a spy mission and hope for the best.

Parking for another hour revealed a wife and kids—a whole world that Dewey never even thought about when it came to teachers. He had this vague notion that teachers stayed in the classrooms where you last left them until you got back.

"Wow!" wondered Dewey. "Do you think he's as boring with his kids? His wife? He can't be . . . Why would anyone marry such a boring guy? She must see *something* in him."

They sat for a while more, and Dewey's stomach started to talk to him about pizza being a lag-free topic. They ordered a medium pepperoni and had it delivered using a nearby home address and intercepting the delivery man. Clara pulled out some kibble for Wolfie, though he sniffed hopefully at the box of pizza.

As they chomped and chewed away, Mr. Nisano eventually came out front with one of the kids they'd seen him with earlier. The little boy was surprisingly cute. He held two fistfuls of toy wooden trains pressed up against his small chest.

"Hold Conductor Tom and make him say something!" implored Mr. Nisano's son.

"Okay," replied Mr. Nisano.

Their play went on for a bit this way, but Mr. Nisano had a newspaper in his hands, and, when he could, he snuck a peek at it to read. The young boy, who couldn't have been much more than three or four years old spoke loudly and clearly.

"Daddy! You're the conductor. Okay? Okay, Daddy? Make him talk now!"

"Oh, the train should not travel that way," narrated Mr. Nisano in the deep make-believe voice of a conductor as he bounced the small wooden man up and down with each word. "There is going to be a storm, I hear." Then, still holding the wooden conductor upright in one hand as if paying attention, he went back to his newspaper.

The boy got distracted for a while in his own play and then looked up to again see his father's eyes on the paper not on him. He tapped him on the shoulder and, when that failed, drove the train across his father's balding head. Dewey and Clara both laughed, and Dewey notated all quickly into his phone.

With the conductor having made his exit from atop his bare head, Mr. Nisano turned the pages of his paper back over themselves and settled nicely into a fresh page. This time, the kid stopped his train play to stand on the lawn. A small arc of water squirted from him like a little hose.

Dewey and Clara burst out laughing. That kid was peeing on his front lawn.

The boy's mother came running out. "What's

going on out here?" she asked Mr. Nisano. "Alexander, Sweetie. That's enough."

"Just playing some trains," he muttered, still looking at the paper.

Little Alexander shot a smile over his shoulder as he finished up his pee.

"I can see that," remarked Mrs. Nisano. "That's enough trains, Alexander. We come inside when we have to make pee pee, okay?" she added as she rested a hand on the top of her son's small head.

Mr. Nisano looked up from his paper, dropping open his mouth but no words came out, and Mrs. Nisano shot her husband a disapproving look. He looked sheepish and flashed her a smile in return, and they all went in the house.

The front door closed, and the stakeout came to an end.

Grh uer fhan

Dewey reviewed his notes in silence as Clara drove him home in time for dinner. She could see from the way his eyebrows worked together, making those three lines of skin between them that looked like a rooster's footprint, that he was busy figuring it all out.

Despite all the pizza, Dewey easily sat with his family for a second dinner and had two servings of grilled chicken, a plate full of broccoli, and a couple of roasted potatoes.

So. Mr. Nisano also has a family. Dewey sat looking at his notes upstairs after dinner. Mr. Nisano has a life, kids, and is sort of a regular guy.

Dewey tossed and flipped his phone around in his hand. His dad *hated* when he did that. "Your phone is not a toy," he'd say. "It's a small computer."

Dewey sat there tossing it a few more times, chuckling as he thought about Mr. Nisano's kid peeing on the front lawn. He tossed his phone and missed catching it, and it dropped to the ground. Carpet. No problem, but he instinctively looked over his shoulder for his dad anyway.

He resumed his rhythmic tossing of his phone, trying to sum up his observations. Mr. Nisano likes his kid. He likes the newspaper.

"I gather he doesn't like trains!" Dewey said aloud and laughed. "He doesn't like trains," he repeated slowly and suspended his phone's acrobatics. "He doesn't like trains! That's it!"

He texted William: Grh uer fhan.

Huh? thought Dewey. *That's weird.* He tried again. The letters still came out all jumbled. Something was wrong with his phone. He tried a hard restart but no good. The letters still came out all jumbled.

He went to his computer and texted William from there instead.

> got our plan
> meet in the office tomorrow at noon

Then he started a search on the computer to find out if it was possible that dropping his phone could have damaged it.

The screen looked fine. No cracks. He dropped it on

carpet. What he read did not encourage him though.

His face started to feel hot as he read more about the delicate nature of smartphones. Words like "fragile components" began to stress him out completely. Dropping your smartphone, it seemed, had a handful of possible outcomes, but very few of those outcomes were ever good.

"Oh, man! Oh, man, oh man, oh man!" Dewey couldn't imagine telling his dad that he had dropped his phone, let alone confessing that he'd been flipping it around.

He restarted it again and tried texting Colin to test it: Testing

It had worked! His face grew hot again as relief replaced his sinking sense of queasy despair. His tummy settled when Colin's text back was equally free of error.

What

Dewey answered him. Dropped my phone! checking if it still works

After he confirmed Dewey's test, Colin sent a meme of a kid laying on his bed accidentally dropping a phone on his own face.

Dewey laughed and sighed.

At noon on Sunday, William came sliding into the office, right on time, to find Clara and Dewey waiting to meet him. William's father was born in India and his mother in Germany. He and his sister were born in America.

The top of his head reached about Dewey's chest. He had thick eyebrows that hung like fuzzy, black caterpillars over his large, warm brown eyes. Today, like most days, he wore a plain white t-shirt with blue jeans. He sat before them, his hair still flattened from his late Sunday morning sleep.

"Good day, William." Dewey pulled his chair closer to his desk as he greeted his client formally. "After thinking over your problem, we've come up with a plan of action.

"As you know, Mr. Nisano is perhaps one of the most boring men on the planet," outlined Dewey. He got up from his chair and began to pace. "So we are going to give him a taste of his own medicine."

"Huh? How do you mean?" William asked with intrigue.

Clara offered William some cookies, sliding the plate toward him. Surprisingly, he politely shook his head and mouthed silently, *No, thank you.*

"No one likes boredom, not even Mr. Nisano. We are going to make sure Mr. Nisano finds himself bored stiff in his own class so that he can't help but get the message."

"Oh, I think I get it, sort of," nodded William slowly, and he reached over mindlessly for a cookie. "But how?"

"We'll take care of that," reassured Dewey. "Just make sure that you do whatever you get prompted to do. Follow our lead. We'll handle the rest."

William left, without much detail about the plan, and Clara raised her chin and eyes to look up at Dewey. "Well, I guess we have our work cut out for us."

"We sure do."

It's a Terrible
Thing to Waste

"I've been thinking. Do you think removing the vending machines relates somehow to the t-issue?" proposed Seraphina as she and Colin brainstormed at her kitchen table.

Seraphina raised her socked feet up on the table as she leaned back in her chair. Colin had his shoes off as well, but he didn't think he should put his feet up on someone else's table, so he stretched his legs out beneath it, his colorful socked feet tapping together like a butterfly expanding and drying its wings before its first flight.

"I can't really see how it would." replied Colin. "I mean the t-issue seems to be about waste and resources. They've got to be making money on those machines, don't they?"

"I don't know," replied Seraphina. "We need to find out why they're taking them both. It just seems weird timing, if you ask me."

"So what do we do? I've got all this information about toilet paper that I wanted you and Dewey to help me use with Mrs. Mayoral. We didn't evolve from using corn cobs and clay to the modern luxury of two-ply paper just to have them dispense it in itty-bitty-minus-cule-meager-pint-sized-stunted pieces! Humans ought not stand in the way of that kind of progress!"

Seraphina laughed. "We can still help you with that," she assured him. She took her feet off the table, removed her sweatshirt, and got some ice water from the refrigerator. Peewee slowly pulled up from under the table to follow her.

"Want some?" she asked as the ice fell noisily into the cup.

"Naw." Colin replied. "Hey, I didn't even know he was under there."

"He's kind of hard to miss," Seraphina chuckled, sticking an ice cube in his large mastiff mouth. Peewee swallowed it whole. He would have gladly sat his full 150-pound, apricot-furred self on her lap if she'd sat on the ground with him, but she sat back in her chair, so he retreated to a cushion the size of a small kiddie pool in the living room.

"Let's do this," she continued, sitting back down with her glass and smoothing out the hair she'd fuzzed up when she removed her sweatshirt. "You draft a letter about why this t-issue is unacceptable. Be sure you do more research though. You have to balance your argument, you know? It can't be all emotion. You need to get some facts in there too."

"Yeah, I can do that. I already have some. I know just where to look for more," replied Colin, "I'm going to prove this t-issue is top-shelf, dude."

"Ha! Good! I'm going to talk to Shawn and see what I can find out about the vending machines."

"What about Dewey?" asked Colin.

"We can catch him up tomorrow at school," she replied. "He's busy working on that case. Besides, I know he'll throw himself into this when he can. No one loves those vending machines more than Dewey."

"That's true," smiled Colin. "I don't think Dewey could actually live without them. I'm serious. It might stop his perspiration completely."

Seraphina laughed again. "I don't think you mean 'perspiration.' I think you mean *respiration. And* I don't think anyone ever died from a vending machine."

"Oh, yeah. Right, respiration. It says here that three men have died!"

"From a vending machine, not perspiration, I assume?"

Colin laughed as he looked back at the article to read more.

"What's your source?" scoffed Seraphina, grabbing his phone to look instead of waiting for him to answer.

Colin tried to grab it back away from her.

"Just wait!" she yelped, trying to read.

"Alright, alright. Here you go," she conceded, handing it back to him. "That's pretty funny. Well, it's awful, of course. I'm just amazed it's true, that's all. They must have been crushed. There's no way they died lamenting the loss of one."

"We must never doubt the genius mind of Colin the Great," he announced putting his socked feet up on the table. "It's a terrible thing to waste."

"Ha! You don't say?!" smiled Seraphina. "I'll keep that in mind. I wo—"

"Wait-a-minute," beamed Colin. "'It's a terrible thing to waste.' That can be our first t-issue slogan."

"I'm not following," she replied. "Isn't that what *they're* concerned about? Waste?"

"Well, it depends on what kind of waste! It works both ways, get it?"

"Um. No."

"Holy Narwhal, Seraphina! Don't you get it?! What do you call the sanitation station?"

"The sanitation station."

"Another name."

"A was—t . . . Oh! A waste treatment plant?! Eww. Waste! That kind. Oh, we can't do that! Can we?"

"It's too good not to! It's got both sides' concerns in one sentence, ours and theirs! How often does that happen?!"

"'T-ISSUE: It's a terrible thing to waste.' It's perfection!" Colin enthusiastically approved his own idea as he packed up his stuff to go home and work on his research. "You'll talk to Shawn?" he asked.

Seraphina agreed to do it as soon as she got to school in the morning.

"Maybe 'It's a Terrible Way to Waste' works better," she suggested, still trying to improve it in her own head.

"Yes! That might make perfection even more perfect," he had to acknowledge.

Seraphina said perfect couldn't be more perfect, because that's what it means to be "perfect," but she appreciated his vote of confidence.

"I wonder how things are going for Dewey?" she asked as Colin departed. *I sure hope he can meet us for lunch tomorrow*, she thought.

Donkeys

Peering through the glass window at the top of the door, Dewey could hear Mr. Nisano speaking to his students.

"Weren't the first chapters of *The Outsiders* marvelous?" he was saying. "There you discovered a world of violence, passion, warring factions, and yes, even romance. Shall we dig into it more today and really get our proverbial feet wet? Our first vocabulary term, then, is 'editorial.'" He spelled it out as he wrote it on the SMART Board. "E-d-i-t-o-r-i-a-l," and he hit the board so hard to punctuate that he'd finished it, Dewey felt certain he'd blunted the tip of his marker. "An 'editorial' is an article in the newspaper, like an opinion piece where the writer gives his or her point of view. The Socs,

I'm sure you recall, get written up in ed-i-tor-ials for helping folks one day and being a nuisance the next.

"Let's go on to the next word, then. 'Loping,'" he called out as he wrote on the board, "is to run or move with long, bounding strides. Please look on page seven. You see? Where he *lopes* to his car?"

As Mr. Nisano droned on and on, students' heads slumped down on their desks, and the others had a faraway look in their eyes.

Dewey wondered where they went when they got that marble-eyed stare. They were present, but not there. Didn't Mr. Nisano notice that they were so far away?

Dewey spotted Olivia, the greatest burper in seventh grade. Man, could she let one rip. Her super long, beautiful black hair and pretty face, round like the moon when full, were easily recognizable. Dewey had always loved his preschool days with her and how they'd run around like crazy, climbing trees and chasing pretend ducks. Now, though, she sat in her seat, chin tilted to one side, lips slightly parted, and her eyes like two stagnant pools of water—she no longer looked like the same Olivia. It was as if her soul had escaped leaving an empty vessel. Ugh! Dewey couldn't take it anymore. It was spooky.

He turned away. Only two more minutes and the plan would go into effect.

Dewey stood at the door with a paper bag filled with

little notes. He had picked this class period because it coincided with his study hall. In fact, he hadn't even had to give his teacher his prepared excuse. She had been speaking on the phone with a counselor, and she nodded and waved him out without taking her attention from the phone.

As the students exited Mr. Nisano's classroom, Dewey handed each one a small note with information detailing the plan. To put anything in writing risked leaving a trail, but Dewey felt confident that this class of kids were desperate for a solution and would take precautions not to give anything away.

He had taken one safety measure though. Just in case, he'd written the directions in disappearing ink. That had been Clara's idea. The pen lasted for about an hour before it started to fade away. It seemed prudent to make their instructions disappear; they'd decided he could count on the kids to remember what to do.

On the paper, in very small font it read:

If you are sick and tired of feeling bored in Mr. Nisano's class, please follow these directions: Whenever you speak in class, do it as slowly as possible and in the least interesting manner possible. Shred this document. More info soon. DF, #teacherproblemsolver

Students read and commented on the small bits of paper as they walked down the hall. Some were laughing. Others shared high-fives. Still others just kept rereading the paper, pointing and whispering. Everyone shredded their note though, and Dewey ran behind and picked up the scraps from the few kids not mindful enough to shove it in their pocket for parents to find later mixed in with the dryer lint.

William's note, however, was not written in disappearing ink. His note had instructions to follow long after the ink disappeared. Dewey trusted that William would take care not to get caught. After all, Dewey's clients all wanted their problems solved *quietly*, and he had made sure none of them had ever been caught.

Ironically, *acting* out the boredom that his students usually suffered so miserably finally gave his class something entertaining to do. The students had a great time seeing who could speak the most monosyllabically and who could keep their answers the flattest and most dull.

The second day of his students rolling along like a bunch of flat tires, Mr. Nisano, usually a pretty flat person himself, blew up. When he called on Olivia, she read the assigned journal entry on the topic of her experience with reputation.

"Good," she read.

"Good?" he asked.

She nodded once.

"Just 'good'? No elaboration? No explanation?"

"Good," she said.

What made it more infuriating for him, perhaps, was that she uttered the single word as if she had answered the question thoughtfully, without a hint of irony or disrespect in her voice.

He sighed and moved on. "Hector, you're up," he said.

"Bad, but I don't feel good about it." Hector read.

Mr. Nisano looked at Hector with raised eyebrows, encouraging him to continue.

Nothing.

He moved on to Nina.

"Hmm? Sorry, what?" she asked in a distracted confusion.

"Dan?"

"Sir?"

"Your entry!"

Dan yawned, and a hiccup-burp slipped out as he slowly flipped back and forth in his notebook, half-heartedly looking for the correct page.

"What is the matter with you people? This is the most tiresome, tedious, yawn-inducing, dull drove of donkeys I've ever encountered!"

William's cue! Reaching into his binder, William pulled out the note card Dewey prepared. It was the closest Dewey could get to his teleprompter idea.

"Um, Mr. Nisano," William raised his hand tentatively in response to the teacher's outburst.

He had Mr. Nisano's attention, so William forged on tentatively. "With all due respect, which you deserve as our teacher—" William felt his heart racing and watched Mr. Nisano.

"Yes, what is it, Mr. Sanai? Your deference is noted. Out with it, already."

"Well, it's just that, well . . ." As he swallowed, somewhere in some other part of his brain he thought to himself, *wow, people really do gulp when they're nervous.* He looked down and read straight from Dewey's card.

"Now you know how we feel."

No laughter resulted. No giggles. William noticed a soft hum coming from the lights above and wished he could disappear into the back of his chair.

Mr. Nisano walked away from the front of the class to his desk, where he leaned his bottom back against the front edge. He reached back to grasp the sides, and uttered, "Huh."

He got that glazed, distant look in his eyes as if he were somewhere else, rather than here in the classroom with them. He looked through them. He looked over them. He nodded his head slowly and repeated, "Huh."

The bell rang, and for the first time ever, no one spoke as they left the class. What, they wondered, could possibly come next?

Dewey Gets Busy

The bell rang for break, and Dewey headed straight for the vending machines. His mom had packed him a snack bar today. The vending machines had snack bars too. He wished she would stop packing him a snack. He told her not to, but she kept doing it anyway.

He bought a pack of roasted almonds. Just as they dropped with a thud, Colin slid in next to him. "Well, my friend, I hope you're going to enjoy those because they could very well be your last."

"No way! They're not taking these machines away. I'll tie myself to one, and they'll have to take me with it first."

"Haha!" Colin grabbed Dewey's backpack and picked him up off the ground with it. "I think they can pull that off pretty easily."

"Hey," Dewey laughed and kicked out of Colin's grasp. "Cut that out! Catch me up on stuff," Dewey said as he popped an almond in his mouth.

"I'm still waiting to hear if Seraphina found out anything from Shawn yet. Are you done with your case yet? Can you come over after school today?"

"Too much homework today, but tomorrow I can. I gotta meet with Clara first, but I can come over after that."

"I'll tell Seraphina that we should meet a little later. Will your parents let you stay for dinner so we can get more planning time?"

"I'll ask," replied Dewey, shaking the salt and crumbs from the almond bag into his mouth. "They sure don't make these packs very big." He felt around in his backpack for his snack bar.

"Where *is* Seraphina?" he added.

"I hope she's getting us information," replied Colin. "Okay, I gotta go!" He pulled out one of the rolls of toilet paper Dewey had given him.

"Ha!" Dewey laughed. "Okay. Don't get lost in there!"

"See ya later."

When Dewey arrived at the office after school the next day, he began to wonder if he would have time to meet with Clara and still go see Colin. Dewey just wanted to sleep in late! When was he supposed to find the time to do that?

Mr. Nisano's classes reported today that he had told a knock-knock joke ("Knock knock," "Who's there?" "Centipede." "Centipede who?" "Centipede on my Christmas tree."). It was the same joke each class period—but it was a start. He began to speak less monotonously too. He even moved the desks out of rows and into a semicircle "to shake things up a bit." The class couldn't believe it, and William called Dewey a genius.

"More cases, Boss," reported Clara.

"Teacher won't let him chew gum?" Dewey read and rolled his eyes. "This one's upset her teacher is a bad dresser!" Some of these weren't real problems, and some of the problems the petitioners would just have to figure out by themselves.

Some issues struck them as more pressing, and Clara had put Bailey's on the top of the pile for just that reason. A fear of swimming had begun to develop for Bailey and her entire class.

"Can you please DM Bailey that we will see her in the next couple of days, and send her some paperwork to get back to us first," Dewey requested. "I gotta run over to Colin's now. We've got a big problem at school with the vending machines. I think they want to get rid of them. Can you imagine? I'll die, Clara. I swear I'll DIE. There's just no reason to be at that school without the vending machines."

"Oh, that's unfortunate. Most injurious, sir. I'm sure you three will hit upon a good solution."

"I sure hope so." Dewey hopped onto the Gator. "Launch me a cookie, would ya?" Dewey added, "please and thank you!" He flashed a smile at Clara as the Gator began to slowly lift him up. Clara tossed him one and then a second cookie.

When he left, Clara sat down at Dewey's desk and chewed slowly on one of her own cookies. Wolfie hopped up and snuggled in next to her, and she patted him on the head, but her mind was a million miles away.

Corn Chips Grow from Corn Seeds

When Dewey arrived, Seraphina and Colin had eaten two slices of pizza each, and Colin was just digging into his third.

"Oh good! You made it!" he said, folding the slice of pizza lengthwise and taking a bite that amounted to about half of it. "Serraphhiaa wooln't ell (chew, chew) anyhing (gulp) until you got here."

Dewey grabbed a slice of pizza, then he thought of Colin's appetite, went back, and placed a second one on his plate before sitting down on the couch.

"The situation is not good," began Seraphina. "But at least I think I know what's going on now. I don't think it's so unrelated to the t-issue, after all."

"What?" Dewey asked. "What did you find out?"

"It's true. They want to get rid of the vending machines. They—"

Before she could finish, Dewey interrupted her and threw himself down onto the floor, rolling around like a toddler having a tantrum. "No! No! No! No!" he cried, thrashing his head back and forth with each denial.

Colin laughed heartily at Dewey's display of wretchedness. Then he swiped a slice of Dewey's pizza.

"Colin!" Seraphina tried to defend Dewey's imperiled dinner provisions.

Her intervention was unnecessary, however, as Dewey swiped it just as quickly back out of Colin's hand.

"Nice try, Cowboy!" he drawled, not even bothering to put the slice back on his plate. Instead, he sent it directly into his mouth.

Colin laughed.

"Seraphina," Dewey began, looking back at her. "This is serious."

"Well, *I* know that," she declared rather exasperatedly. "You two Sasquatch need to focus!"

"Seraphina, I'm totally focused. Colin. Focus," he guided, putting one hand on each of Colin's shoulders. Colin nodded to indicate he had settled down.

"It's all part of some bigger plan for 'Ecological Awareness' that the school is working on. There is some committee that comes in and reviews schools, and the reviewers reported weaknesses in our district."

"So that's why we're skimping on toilet paper?" asked Colin.

"Yes, it seems so. They'll be replacing the paper towels with air driers soon too," added Seraphina.

"Ugh. I hate drying my hands with those driers, but I can live with that. Is it really asking so much for my paper to roll out at least three pieces at a time, though?" he demanded. He spoke with his hands palms up and fingers spread, as if each hand held a roll of triple-ply as he shrugged.

"What about the vending machines? How do they fit in?" Dewey ignored Colin's theatrics.

"According to Shawn, they want us to grow our own snacks."

"They want us to—what?!" Colin's hands flew up again, this time up over his head.

"You heard me. Students plant our own garden. We plant the seeds, we water them, plants grow, and we eventually eat them. They want one this winter and one again in the spring"

"We could grow old and starve to death waiting for all that!" howled Dewey.

"Are we supposed to grow our own corn chips?"

"No," Seraphina shook her head. "Just grow the corn."

Dewey got up and started pacing. "This is worse than I thought."

"When?" asked Colin.

"I'm not sure," Seraphina sighed. "I guess we'll find out soon enough."

V-Ending Machine

If by "soon enough" Seraphina meant tomorrow, she would have been correct. The next day when Dewey got to school, he felt as if someone had swiftly kicked him in the stomach. They were gone. Before he even had time to think about how to stop it, the vending machines, the things he enjoyed most about middle school, ceased to be.

There, in their place, sat an information table with parent volunteers. They had "healthy snack" information packets for kids to take home to their parents and face painting.

"Face painting!" cried Dewey to Seraphina. "What in the fruit loops does face painting have to do with any of this?"

"Hey! Dewey!" Dewey and Seraphina looked over and discovered Colin getting his face painted. He was explaining to the volunteer painter that a narwhal was a large-tusked whale. She told him she wasn't so good at whales and suggested he might like a large tusk-like carrot painted on his cheek instead.

"You look ridiculous," laughed Dewey when Colin was finished, and they walked away from the table. Colin had an almost life-sized carrot painted on the side of his face.

"Yeah," he acknowledged. "I wanted a narwhal!"

"Who told you to go get your face painted, you noob?" Dewey could always count on Colin to cheer him up, even in a crisis.

"Hee hee!" Seraphina poked her finger in Colin's orange dimple. "I think Colin's cheek makes a very nice root vegetable. I hope that doesn't wash off too easily. It's a good look."

"Okay, okay!" said Colin.

"We need a plan." Dewey looked at the clock on the wall and groaned. The bell to go back to class would ring any minute.

"I have an orthodontist appointment after school today," reported Seraphina.

"You're getting braces?" asked Colin.

"Not sure yet. They have to decide, I guess."

DEWEY FAIRCHILD, TEACHER PROBLEM SOLVER

"Welcome to the orthodontic club," and Colin flipped his retainer in his mouth like a somersault.

"That's just gross," cried Seraphina. "And why is it blue?"

"You can get any color you want," Colin dangled it between his thumb and pointer finger.

"Well, park it on the roof of your mouth, will you?"

"I can't meet either," interrupted Dewey, oblivious to their banter. He really needed to meet with Bailey. "How about we just text later tonight?"

The bell rang.

They all agreed and went off to class. Dewey still laughing at Colin's carrot face but also with an empty feeling in his stomach—not just because he hadn't eaten a snack today.

Perfect, Thin, and Crispy

According to Bailey's questionnaire, her teacher problem stemmed from his obsession with sharks. School had been in session for only a couple of months, and that's all they talked about every day.

When she slid into the office Sunday, Dewey had not yet arrived. Wolfie greeted her with whining and talking.

Clara had him on a leash because lately he had been acting like he ran the roost, and she was having none of that.

"Wolfie, no," Clara admonished as Wolfie gave a high-pitched yelp, begging Bailey to rub his haunches.

"Aww, he's so adorable," smiled Bailey, petting him.

Bailey Campos had been in a different elementary school from Dewey, so he did not know her that well. She was Mexican-American with brown, shoulder-length hair. Her warm sienna-brown eyes smiled even before the sides of her upturned mouth reached toward them. She had a reputation for her spirited sense of humor, and she and her friends were a lively and giggle-some bunch.

"Yes, yes, I know," smiled Clara. "I just would prefer it if he didn't jump up and demand affection. It's unbecoming," she stressed as she looked Wolfie straight in the eye. He, in response, rubbed up against Bailey's leg, eliciting another rub from her.

"Dewey should be here any moment now," Clara filled in the momentary silence. "Please, have a seat. I have some cookies just coming out of the oven. I hope you like french fries," she called out over her shoulder as she attended to her baked goods.

French fries? wondered Bailey. *That's weird.* She sat and played with Wolfie while she waited. She couldn't believe how soft and silky Wolfie's black and white fur felt, more like a cat's than a dog's. Bailey had just stood up to look for a ball or something to throw for Wolfie when Dewey slid into the office.

"Hey, Bailey! Sorry I'm late."

"No problem. I've been hanging out with Wolfie."

She smiled and rubbed Wolfie's back. "Isn't that right, Wolfie?" she cooed.

Dewey sat at his desk and opened his notes from Bailey's case. He had reviewed them last night, but he and Clara had not had a chance to go over them yet.

"So," Dewey wanted to confirm with her, "I've read it all, but let me hear the main issues from you."

"Well, for one," replied Bailey, "we're getting sharked-out! It's boring to only study one thing all year long! But I guess the bigger thing is, well, um, he shows us these movies on sharks, and they're freaking us out. I refuse to swim in the ocean anymore." Bailey looked around cautiously as if the walls had ears and lowered her voice, "I don't even want to take a bath!"

When Clara walked in, Dewey's nose registered the sweet smell of cookies. When he looked up, she handed them salted fries in a wax paper packet. Suddenly, his senses felt mixed up.

"Um, Clara? French fry cookies?"

"Yes, sir!"

"Ah! Guests first!" laughed Dewey, nodding for Bailey to try a fry first.

Bailey took one and smiled big.

Clara had made sugar cookie strips, with grains of sugar to look like salt flakes, packaged in a white paper french fry bag. Each bag came with vanilla and chocolate dipping sauces dyed red with pomegranate juice to look like ketchup.

"Nice, Clara! Very nice!" approved Dewey.

Clara nodded and headed off to get the next batch, this time crinkle fries, into the oven.

Dewey pretty much expected everything Bailey had shared, but he hadn't considered that Mr. Snow's class scared kids to that extent they would be afraid to get into their own bathtubs, especially a funny, spunky kid like Bailey.

"Shark anatomy, shark reproduction, shark habitat, shark classification, shark evolution, shark features, shark eating habits, shark communication, shark senses, shark social structure. Did you know there are about 440 known species of sharks, and we have to know them all?" Bailey complained as she flipped through her science binder, showing Dewey each of the required dividers. "Endangered sharks, shark diet, shark behavior."

"So . . . you don't want to take a bath because you're scared of sharks?" he clarified.

"Yeah. I know it's dumb. But I'm not the only one. A couple other kids said the same thing about showering, which makes even less sense. I guess we're just kind of nervous. No one's going to the beach, I can tell you that much."

"Fascinating," replied Dewey. "I wond—" but before

he could finish his thought, Bailey interrupted him.

"Dewey," she continued. "It's worse. I know one kid who won't drink from the water fountain now."

"Whh-oh-oh," responded Dewey, combining "what" and "whoa" into a three-syllable word. He fed a cookie fry into his mouth and then another. "I'm going to need a day or so to work on this.

"In the meantime, ever done a fake bath? Just run the tub, splash a little water from the sink so your hair looks damp, and your mom will think you're in the tub. That should hold you over for a day or two."

Bailey left with a to-go bag of fries and Dewey's assurance that he would be in touch soon.

"Oh!" Dewey called as Bailey crawled out through the ducts. "Don't forget to lock the door when you take your fake bath!" Dewey had learned that from experience.

Dewey sat at his desk thinking about Bailey's case and wondering how to solve something as big as a tiger shark. As he sat there, Wolfie at his feet, he nibbled at a cookie fry and got distracted by the smell of the next batch ready in the oven. What had Clara called it, that word that sounded like a mallard duck?

Clara came back in with the crinkled fries.

"What's that thing, Clara, when the cookie gets that smell in the oven that smells so good—that sounds like the mallard duck effect?"

Clara chuckled. "Maillard Effect. Not mallard duck!" she smiled warmly.

"Right," he nodded. "Okay, help me figure this Mr. Snow thing out, would ya?" He motioned for her to sit down.

"Bailey's teacher? How challenging is it?"

"This guy is obsessed, all right. Totally shark obsessed. He loves sharks more than a five-year-old loves trash trucks. Look at this," he said, flipping through the binder Bailey had left for him. "Worksheets on sharks. Word searches on sharks. Shark lectures. Shark projects. Shark tests."

Clara looked through the material, amazed at what she found.

"Look, here, Boss. He has customized his entire lesson plan—it covers the state standards with only shark-based study! Now that's commitment."

They read the shark-centric syllabus together:

This semester, students will focus on Structure and Function in Living Systems.

The anatomy and physiology of **sharks** illustrates the complementary nature of structure and function. By the end of the semester, successful understanding will require:

1. Students know **sharks** have levels of organization

for structure and function, including cells, tissues, organs, organ systems, and the whole organism.

   a. Students know organ systems function because of the contributions of individual organs, tissues, and cells, and how failure of any part can affect the entire system.

2. Students know how **shark** bones and muscles work together, forming the musculoskeletal system, to provide a structural framework for movement.

3. Students know how the organs of the reproductive system of the **shark** female and male generate eggs and sperm and know how sexual activity may lead to fertilization and pregnancy.

   a. Students know the structure and function of the umbilicus and placenta during **shark** pregnancy.

4. Students know how to relate the structures of the **shark** nervous system, including the eyes and ears, to their functions.

"Man, this guy really *is* obsessed. Well, here's something to sink your teeth into, if we don't want kids afraid to swim, or worse yet, to grow up thinking that babies come from sharks, we'd better figure out how to solve this problem."

Dewey grabbed a crinkle fry and sat quietly thinking. This time, instead of just slipping the whole cookie into his mouth, he nibbled on each ridge of the cookie-fry. He found it satisfying to have his front and bottom teeth drive over the flat part of the cookie until the front teeth hit the ridge, where he slowly bit down, savoring how it tasted buttery and perfect each time. He began to think about that weird way taste buds register it so ridiculously good when butter and sugar come together. Clara was pretty clever, turning all that sweet deliciousness into faux french fries.

Then came the breakthrough idea that had nothing to do with Bailey or sharks.

"Clara," he muttered slowly. "If you can make cookies that look like french fries, you can make cookies that look like carrots too, right?"

"Well, sure, Boss. You can make something look like anything, really."

"Something look like anything. Something look like anything! That's IT! Clara, we're going to save the school!" He grabbed and hugged her hard. Clara, who hadn't gotten hugs from Dewey for a while now, felt grateful to feel his warmth and enthusiasm.

"Well, that's great, sir. Anything to help, you know that."

"I gotta go. I need to tell Seraphina and Colin! See

if you can figure out how we're going to help Bailey. I have no idea how to navigate shark-infested waters in a bathroom!"

"Yes. On it. Thinking cap going on," and she mimed putting a winter cap on her head. "Until tomorrow."

And off Dewey went to share his idea with his friends and see if they thought it might, just might, work.

When Dewey entered, he discovered Seraphina flopped across her bed. Her head hung down over the edge with her face toward the mattress, and her long curly brown hair looked like strands of thick coiled rope. Colin lay on the carpet, his knees up, staring at the ceiling.

Dewey grabbed a pencil off the desk and used it to lift one of the strands up into itself.

"Well, this is a productive team," he teased.

"We are on a think break," replied Seraphina, her face and voice muffled by the bed.

"Y-up," contributed Colin, still staring at the ceiling.

Dewey just stood there waiting for them to say something. Anything.

Nope. Nothing.

"Guys, you seem to have hit a wall or something."

"Yes," declared Seraphina, lifting her pointer finger in assent. She also tried to lift her head as the blood rushing to it made it feel like fifty pounds, but then decided it took more effort than she wanted to exert. "A wall," she agreed, lowering both finger and head back down.

"Y-up," yawned Colin.

"Sit up, you two. I've got a plan."

"What? Really?" Seraphina swung her body and head up from the edge of the bed to sit with crossed legs. "Colin, Dewey has a plan! Really?" she asked again, looking at Dewey and sitting up tall.

"Really," he reiterated. "Colin! Get up!" He poked Colin's hip with the eraser side of the pencil.

"Okay, okay, let's hear it," Colin said as he scooted himself up and rested his back against Seraphina's dresser.

Dewey told them all about how Clara's cookie fries and how it had given him the idea. If the school seemed so set on them growing this garden themselves, then they'd just take the garden back into their own hands. He told them his vision for a vending machine garden.

"This is good," admitted Colin. "Really good."

"Yes," agreed Seraphina. "We need more details."

"Thank you, thank you. You guys gotta think of some good ideas now."

Seraphina nodded her head several times.

"Oh yeah. I just need some time to get my brain going. But now thinking is fun again and doesn't hurt my head so much."

"Good," said Dewey.

"What about your t-issue, though?" Seraphina addressed Colin. "How does that fit into all of this?"

"Oh, don't worry," Colin assured her. "I'm not letting all that work we've done go down the drain!"

"Haha!" laughed Dewey.

Colin laughed too. "Good one!"

"Yeah, good one," acknowledged Seraphina, "but aren't we supposed to say that?"

"My dad always says, 'you need to be able to laugh at your own jokes in case nobody else does.' Of course, his jokes are usually pretty bad, so there's that."

"Yeah," agreed Seraphina smiling. "There's that."

"Okay!" Dewey clapped his hands together and stood up. "We've got a plan. At least we're on our way. Take away the vending machines," he grumbled. "Hmph! I don't think so!"

Stick Figuring

Dewey couldn't believe what he observed during his research Monday. Kids coming out of Mr. Snow's science class afraid to drink from the water fountain, some even afraid to use their water bottles!

"They're going to get dehydrated," Dewey reported to Clara. "I don't know where to start."

"I imagine you'll begin with why he's so obsessed with sharks," suggested Clara, handing Dewey a chocolate cookie.

"Right," replied Dewey. He fixed himself to hypothesize on the shark issue when he hit the center of the cookie. "Whoa! Peppermint Patty?!" he exclaimed, astonished.

"Yup. Snuck them right in there. Good idea, no?"

"No. I mean, yes! Why do people say no when they mean yes?"

"Why, indeed?" twinkled Clara as she sat down across from him and began to sketch out a picture.

"Here you've got your teacher," she drew a stick figure. "And your class of students," she continued with some Xs and Os with curly hair, straight hair, or hats. "Now," she paused. "Sharks." She drew little fish with big sharp teeth all over the page and tapped her pencil tip as she appeared to contemplate.

Then she turned the page over. "Before this scene," she continued, "there must have been another," and she drew another stick figure teacher, a toothy fish, and a big question mark inside the round head of the stick figure teacher. "Because," she said, offering Dewey another chocolate cookie, "sometimes the inside of a cookie just might surprise you."

Concentric Circles

Dewey's dad would always say, "I'm not grumpy," when it was as big as life to everyone that he was, most surely, surly.

"Something in the kitchen stinks," Stephanie complained as she breezed past the kitchen sink to grab toast out of the toaster.

"Don, did you take out the trash last night?" asked Dewey's mom from the bathroom brushing her teeth.

"What?" he asked.

"Stalling," replied Dewey's mom. Dewey's dad always said "what" when he didn't have a good answer lined up.

"No, really, Karen, I didn't hear you."

"Mom wants to know if you took out the trash," Stephanie chimed in.

"I heard her," growled Dewey's dad.

He went to the kitchen and took out the garbage.

"You know," he directed his chin and words at Dewey, who sat at the table eating cereal when his dad came back in, "you could take out the trash sometimes."

Oh boy, thought Dewey. *I gotta get out of here.*

Dewey's mom came out of the bathroom and patted Dewey on the head. "It's true. You could start taking out the trash sometimes. But it wasn't your job last night," she reassured him, pressing her hand on top of his. "Don, you're obviously distressed about something. What's on your mind?"

"Nothing," pouted Dewey's dad, and he sat down and slumped his face in his hands, so his whole family would know for sure it was something.

"Karen, rub my back, would you?" Dewey's dad like his back rubbed in big concentric circles when he felt upset about something.

"There, there," cooed Dewey's mom. "Whatever it is will be okay. Were the big kids mean to you at school?" she asked, smiling.

"Kind of," moped Dewey's dad, but he smiled now.

"Really?" asked Dewey, intrigued.

"No, not really. They're fine. I just have a lot of papers to grade and a lot of my own homework to do," his dad grumbled. "I'll live. I just can't wait until winter break!"

"Ha! That makes two of us," agreed Dewey.

"Me three," agreed Stephanie.

"Me three too," chimed in Pooh Bear, licking her fingers after sucking on a sausage.

"Okay, well, how about you three clear your places, please, so we're not late for school."

Leave for school already?! *Shoot*. Dewey had hoped to spend a few minutes on Mr. Snow's background search. *Ack!* thought Dewey. *Too many balls in the air!* One was bound to drop.

Gratitude

During study hall, Dewey decided to focus on getting his homework done, so later that evening he could focus on some of his other work.

He told his parents he had a lot of homework, and since his dad did too, the two of them got excused from after dinner clean up and went off to work. *Well,* Dewey rationalized, *this certainly constituted work and he was at home.*

Dewey first looked up on his school's website to find the staff list to get Mr. Snow's first name. Brad. Brad Snow. *He looks like a Brad,* thought Dewey, his mind's eye filling in where the camera's lens cut off. If Mr. Snow's entire body appeared instead of Ms. Webster's headshot below him, Brad Snow's bearded head would sit atop a square. He wore jeans, a collared, button-down shirt—always some shade of blue—and boat shoes. Yes, short and stocky, but solid of body and mind. He ran a tight ship, in-baskets, out-baskets, pen cups, staplers, everything labeled with his Baby Label Maker. He kept his brown beard trimmed close and hair neatly parted. *Weird how people can look or not look like their names.*

Dewey wondered if he looked like a Dewey. He felt like a Dewey. He couldn't imagine any other name for himself, really. Dewey didn't know any other Deweys. Take a name like Colin, though. Lots of Colins ran around, and none of them seemed at all like one another. Yet somehow, Colin "felt" like a Colin to him. Did those other Colins feel like Colins too, once you got to know them? Did they feel like Colins to themselves? Or did they wake up each day feeling like someone else had their name—maybe Nash, or Aiden, or Lukas?

Dewey brought his thoughts back to the present task and did some searches on Brad Snow. He showed up along with some other Brad Snows—a football player, some poster artist, a real estate agent. Dewey also found some Bradley Snows, so he followed those as well with some overlap. From what he could tell, his Brad Snow had taught in a couple different schools and had grown up here. He had a Facebook page which had good privacy settings because Dewey couldn't get in beyond his profile pictures. He owned a home.

It took some time, but he finally hit his mark when he entered "Bradley Snow shark attack" as a search.

His name didn't come up, but someone else with the last name Snow did. A Timothy Snow lost his hand to a shark seven years ago. The article reported that he'd been preparing for a triathlon by swimming early mornings in the ocean. The water had been cold, and he swam in a wet suit and flippers. The shark, the experts concluded, must have mistaken him for a seal, and it took a chunk out of Timothy's right arm. He had also lost his right hand.

Whoa, thought Dewey. *This can't be a coincidence.* He did a search for "Bradley Snow siblings" but that didn't work. Then he tried it the other way around: "Timothy Snow siblings." Nothing. There had to be some way to establish that Timothy Snow was related to Bailey's Mr. Snow.

Dewey read some more articles about Timothy Snow. He learned a lot more about the incident, but none of the articles mentioned a brother or Bradley Snow.

He tried just researching Timothy Snow. *I'll try his social media.* And there he appeared—right on Instagram. Timothy Snow had pictures of Mr. Snow. Cousins maybe? Probably brothers. Mr. Snow had a shark obsession because someone he loved got chewed up by one!

Dewey wanted to tell Clara what he'd discovered, but he looked at the time, and it read half past ten. He felt surprised, come to think of it, that no one had come to tell him to turn off the lights yet.

Dewey tiptoed to the bathroom to get ready for bed. Suddenly, for the first time ever, he appreciated his right hand and how hard it would be to floss without it. Weird, he'd never thought about that before. He flossed and brushed his teeth then padded off to bed.

Galeophobia

When Dewey came in after school Tuesday, carrots, broccoli, green snow pea pods, zucchini, and red bell peppers covered his desk.

Wolfie, alert and staring, positioned himself right in front of Clara's feet. Wolfie loved carrots, but he loved cookies even more, and each and every one of these vegetables was just that.

"Amazing!" Dewey marveled as he held a zucchini in his hand and gently turned it around.

"They're just prototypes," Clara noted.

"They're perfect! Can I show them to Colin and Seraphina?"

Clara nodded, her cheeks turning a shade of red just short of her bell pepper cookies.

Clara stacked them up carefully for Dewey in a plastic Tupperware container. "Just be sure I get my Tupperware back. That's real Tupperware. We used to have to go to parties to get these, you know."

"Tupperware *parties*?" Dewey asked incredulously.

"Yes! Tupperware parties."

"Boy, you sure knew how to have a good time, Clara!" Before she could reply, Dewey switched to a more thoughtful tone. "Hey, Clara, I figured out the Mr. Snow thing. His brother—or cousin maybe, but I think it's his brother, looks like him—anyway, a shark attacked him about seven years ago!"

Clara stood nodding. That made a lot of sense to her. "What's next?"

"Next, I gotta get him to understand he's scaring the pants off his students. I worked late last night. I think I've got the start of a plan."

"Want to tell me now or let me see it unfold, and tell me if you need me?"

"Let's let it unfold. I've got this, the t-issue, the garden, homework, and Mom still keeps thinking I have time to watch Pooh!"

"Unfold it is."

Dewey sat on the floor to give Wolfie some belly rubs. Wolfie made some noises that sounded like "Arr, rrrrarr, rarrrr, rarrrr, rarrrr," to let Dewey know his belly rubs felt marvelous. Somehow, Dewey never felt too busy when he buried his face in Wolfie's belly.

Then Wolfie rolled over, jumped up, and gave a fake sneeze.

"What do you want, Buddy?" Dewey threw his skunk, but Wolfie just stared up at him, still in anticipation of something.

"Oh, the cookies?" Dewey had the Tupperware of vegetable-shaped cookies next to him on the floor.

"No, sorry, Puppy. I'll get you a real carrot, though." Dewey went to Clara's fridge, took out a carrot, and broke it in half. "Here you go, Wolfers. Chew on this for a while." He stuck half the carrot in Wolfie's mouth. The carrot's thickest part was about an inch-and-a-half around, and Wolfie took it over to his bed to work on it like a big chew stick.

"Okay, Clara; I'm off. Talk later. Thank you so much. These look great. I'll give you the go-ahead soon!"

Dewey rode up the Gator and climbed out with the cookies. He walked over to Colin's and knocked at the front door, but no one answered.

He texted Colin: Left the live samples for the garden at your door don't eat! show Seraphina

Colin replied: K

Then he had to run back home to watch Pooh. Dewey's mom had a book club, and Dewey's dad had a class.

"I gave Pooh a snack," reviewed Dewey's mom as she prepared to leave. "I told her you have homework to do, and she has projects to keep her occupied, but you do need to check in on her now and again, okay, Dews?"

"Yup," he agreed.

"I'll be home before dinner, but I'd like the table set, and you can have her help you. Stephanie won't be home until after dinner, so it's just the four of us."

"Yup," Dewey acknowledged.

"Give me a kiss," his mom ordered, pointing to her cheek.

Dewey gave the kiss. He didn't mind kissing her when she asked, but he didn't seem to do it on his own as often these days. She always said, "In our family, we kiss hello and goodbye. Get used to it."

As soon as she left, Dewey wanted to go up and do some more research on the Mr. Snow case. Of course, Pooh Bear had other ideas in store for him.

"Wanna do something with me?" she asked.

"Naw, Pooh, I gotta do homework. Didn't Mom tell you?"

"I don't know."

Oh, she knew. She just wanted to torture him. She always did this. He felt guilty turning her away, and she knew it.

"How about if you work on your—what is it you're

working on?"

"My dollhouse."

"Right. How about you work on your dollhouse for a while, and then in a little bit I can play with you. Could that be okay?"

"Yeah, okay. That could be okay," she agreed and bounced out of the room announcing she'd become a kangaroo.

Dewey sat down to research more about the fear of sharks which he soon learned psychologists called galeophobia.

"Interesting," Dewey said aloud to himself. He'd discovered that one of the main ways to overcome galeophobia is to research sharks. Well, clearly, Mr. Snow was doing a lot of that.

He even showed the students shark entertainment films during his Friday Films at lunch. In *Sharknado* a disaster like a tornado hits Los Angeles, and the ocean spews out shark-infested ocean all over the place. Dewey and his friends couldn't believe they got to watch it at school. The entire premise of the movie seemed totally ridiculous, and not at all educational, but far be it for them to complain about something so great. Limbs got ripped off left and right. Sharks got shot and chainsawed. Blood and guts splattered all over the screen. Dewey and all his friends who didn't even have the class would come in on Fridays to eat their lunch and watch the carnage in Mr. Snow's classroom.

The script was so preposterous that none of the kids outside of Mr. Snow's class got scared—they just laughed and screamed and enjoyed the lunchtime entertainment. But some of Mr. Snow's students had bad dreams after watching it, despite all the diversion it seemed to provide.

Thinking back, Dewey could remember one of them talking about his bad dreams from it.

"I had this dream that when we went to Hawaii, this volcano had sharks spewing out of the lava," Dewey had heard one of the kids telling another kid at lunch after the movie day. "I'm on the sand at the beach, and they start swimming out at me from the water one way, and from the other way, the lava and sharks flow toward me down from the hotel!—I told my parents I don't want to go on that Maui trip with them anymore."

At the time, Dewey didn't give that story much thought; he didn't even really know the kid telling it. He just remembered thinking it was pretty dumb to worry about sharks swimming around in lava considering they would cook before they even got anywhere near you . . . and the fact that no shark had ever seen the inside of a volcano.

All this got Dewey thinking. Mr. Snow's classes

received a lot of shark information and facts, but research about sharks that dispelled the myths about their danger to humans seemed to be missing.

The way Dewey figured it, the two people who would need to fear sharks the most would be fishermen and surfers. They were obviously not afraid—or they were just really stupid—because they were in the water all the time.

So, he sat down and began to discover why they weren't scared to swim in the ocean with sharks, when he suddenly remembered Pooh Bear. She had been awfully quiet.

Dewey went in to check on her and was trying to think of something they might do together that wouldn't take too long. He didn't want to break his promise to her.

When he stuck his head into her room, she wasn't there, so he called out for her. He didn't feel worried as she often got lost deep in her play and didn't reply. When he found her, he let out a small gasp and whispered, "Yes!" to the room, fist bumping the air. She had fallen asleep on their parents' bed.

He pulled a folded afghan off the chair and draped it over her ever-so-gently.

"Yes!" He did a little jig and went back to his computer.

He searched: "Reasons you don't need to fear

sharks," "Fisherman don't fear sharks," "Surfers aren't afraid of sharks." He gathered as much information as he could. Yesterday he was a Dewey who knew very little about sharks. Today, and forevermore, he was a Dewey who knew a lot about sharks.

The house didn't breathe a sound now. Dewey thought about arranging a meeting with Mr. Snow, about organizing Clara's vegetable cookies, about his homework, the vending machine nightmare. His chest got tight and let him know he'd forgotten to exhale. The body, it seemed, had a way of doing that even without his help.

After dinner and dishes, he went back to his room and took his notes, organized them, and emailed Mr. Snow asking for a lunch meeting Thursday. He felt tired, and when his mom told him it was time to wash up for bed, he didn't argue. As he put the toothpaste on his toothbrush, though, he suddenly felt hungry. He'd been getting "peckish," as his dad said, right at bedtime lately. It made his mom mad sometimes because it usually happened after Dewey had already flossed and brushed for the night. She'd usually cut up an apple and tell him to eat that and go to bed. But these days, a cut-up apple wasn't cutting it.

He flashed her a guilty smile.

"Ugh, Dewey. You're going to feel tired in the morning."

Dewey felt in the mood for some eggs and toast.

He went downstairs and fried up an egg in the pan. He knew how to make them better than his mom did now. He'd learned a trick online about putting the lid on the top of the small pan to make a no-flip over easy egg, that way he didn't have to risk breaking the yolk.

He mopped up the warm runny yellow yolk and put some of the egg white onto his buttered sourdough toast. He let out a long, easy sigh. He took a few more bites and scraped up what was left with his fork, licked it clean and set the pan and his dish soaking. Back upstairs, he got ready for bed. The sooner he slept, the sooner he'd wake up and get his meeting arranged and over with. He hoped it would be over easy too! *What had Colin said about laughing at your own jokes?* he smiled to himself. *Where was an audience when you needed one?*

On a Royal Roll

"How may I be of service, Dewey?" asked Mr. Snow as he took a bite of a tuna sandwich.

"Well, Mr. Snow, I've been doing a lot of research on sharks lately, just kind of for fun. And I was wondering if you'd be interested or willing to let me do a presentation on it in your classes."

"Well!" replied Mr. Snow, looking more interested now in Dewey than in his sandwich. "That's just the kind of studentship I'm always looking for around here. What inspired you to take this project on?"

The smell of tuna, while not usually Dewey's kind of sandwich, made his stomach gurgle, and his own peanut butter and jelly sandwich now seemed too sweet in comparison.

"I guess I've always just been curious about sharks, and I could use the service learning credit," answered Dewey. Maybe if he had potato chips with his sandwich it would break it up a bit. His mom had packed crackers, though, which wouldn't do at all. Mr. Snow had potato chips, and he pressed an entire one into his mouth. Dewey wished he could ask Mr. Snow for a couple of chips.

"Well, let's do this!" said Mr. Snow, mouth full of tuna and chips now. "You just tell me when and what you need."

"Okay," answered Dewey. "I'll bring my laptop, so I can just be all set."

"Next week? Monday?"

"Sure," agreed Dewey, now panicking a bit as he thought about how much he had to do between now and then. "Monday. If you need to reach me before you can text me on my cell. I check that more than my email," said Dewey writing it on a sticky note for him.

Mr. Snow put the other half of the sandwich in his mouth. It only took his pointer finger to guide the whole thing in. With his cheek full and round like a ball, he managed to artfully muffle out, "Okay, see you then," without spraying a single fleck of food.

"See you then," repeated Dewey as he gathered up his mostly uneaten lunch and walked out the door.

Before he could even appreciate the sigh of relief he let out, Dewey inhaled, realizing he needed to catch up with his friends and the garden plan.

Dewey looked for Colin and Seraphina in their usual lunch spot but had no luck. He wondered if they might have gone to the garden, and that's exactly where he found them.

"Hey, did you guys know that you're more likely to get crushed by a vending machine then get attacked by a shark?" Dewey added to the conversation as if he'd been there the entire time.

"See?!" said Colin to Seraphina referencing their earlier conversation about death-by-vending machines.

"What? Really? Is that true? That's funny. Where did you come from?" asked Seraphina, looking around.

"Yeah, where have you been?" chimed in Colin.

"Braving the shark-infested waters of room 203," replied Dewey taking a bite of his pb&j. "And uh-huh. It's true. You're also more likely to get bitten by someone in New York than by a shark," added Dewey. "Or a dog. Or a squirrel, for that matter."

Colin laughed.

"You're more likely to die taking a selfie, falling out of bed, or trying to fix your toilet."

"Well, you have been busy," commented Seraphina with admiration in her voice. "Can you help us now?"

"Yeah. I worked late on this shark thing. I'm almost done. I emailed some surfers and fishermen to see if they'd let me interview them this weekend, which would make it SO much better. But it's totally coming together. I got this. I just haven't slept much, but whatever. Sleep is overrated." Dewey grabbed one of Clara's zucchini cookie prototypes and used his finger as Mr. Snow had to bulldoze the entire thing into his mouth.

"Dewey! I've been preventing Colin from doing that for two days!" objected Seraphina.

"Yes. Yes, she has," confirmed Colin, nodding his head profoundly.

Dewey attempted to say, "Catch me up?" but instead ended up laughing and sprayed cookie dust and spittle like a leaf blower—everywhere.

"Dewey!" cried Seraphina again, and Colin laughed. Dewey grabbed a water bottle and washed down the cookie.

"Sorry. So sorry." He put his hand on Seraphina's shoulder to steady himself and put on his most diligent face.

"So," he took another swig of water to focus himself. "Continue."

"We're going to take on the school's plan for a garden," began Seraphina. "We turn the soil, make the rows for the plants to grow, plant the seeds, put in some trellising and some vining plants and even maybe some of those tomato cages."

"Then," chimed in Colin, "when they least expect it, we're going to plant rows and rows of Clara's cookies. Also, we'll clip to all the—what do you call those tick-tack-toe things?" he asked, snapping his fingers.

"Trellises?" offered Dewey.

"Yeah, right, we're going to clip all the vending machine snacks to the trellises and the tomato cages! Snacks will dangle for the picking like ripe fruits and veggies!" Colin's hands swept across the air like a wizard casting a spell.

"Oh," nodded Dewey contemplatively. "This is actually quite good."

"What do you mean, 'actually'?" laughed Colin, feigning indignation. Seraphina blushed, though. They had come far since the days when Dewey had solved the problem of her overprotective mother.

"No," assured Dewey. "It's great! There's only one problem. How are we going to keep the squirrel, birds, and raccoons from eating the cookies?"

"Oh," nodded Colin, reaching for a zucchini. "That's a good point."

"How are we going to keep Colin away?" said Seraphina, slapping his wrist.

"What about if we shock them?" suggested Colin.

"Shock them?!" cried Dewey and Seraphina in unison.

"You know, like we put up an electric shock fence?"

"Those poor little squirrels!" said Dewey, imaging them frying to death trying to reach a carrot cookie. "That's awful."

"We could stake out the place at night with water guns?" he suggested.

"I'm not spending the night spraying water at poor defenseless critters. We'll get caught and the cookies will get all wet," objected Seraphina.

Colin took out his phone, spent a minute looking and then reported, "Got it! The Outdoor Solar Powered Ultrasonic Animal and Pest Repeller."

"Go on," encouraged Dewey.

"It blasts a big ultrasonic noise to scare away a 'wide variety of pests.'"

"Oh, that's good!" nodded Seraphina.

"Cats, raccoons, skunks, dogs, squirrels, and much more."

"Nice," said Dewey.

"Weather proof, environmentally friendly, humane, wireless . . . man, we should start selling these!"

"Are they in stock?" asked Seraphina?

"Yes! Amazon Prime. Can be here the day after tomorrow."

"All right then," nodded Dewey. "We've got a plan! I'll order them when I get back to my office. And the t-issue takes a backseat for the time being?"

"What? No! It's all the same thing. We've got to take our school back! You can't take away our snacks! You can't take away our royal roll!

"Royal *roll*, now?!" laughed Dewey, and Seraphina shrugged.

"Yeah, royal paper, royal roll. Same thing," declared Colin. "A royal pain in the necessity."

"Ha! Okay, then. That gives me an idea, I think," mused Dewey. "Nice work, you two. I'll tell Clara we need, oh, say six hundred cookies in the next couple weeks, and you guys get yourselves involved with the school working on that winter garden!"

Royal roll had given Dewey an idea for a slogan. But his mind now turned to another thought. The Outdoor Solar Powered Ultrasonic Animal and Pest Repeller might be just the added assurance they needed around their office for those mice. He would order two extra.

Community Service

Mr. Snow's classes raved over Dewey's presentations the next Monday. Dewey presented "Shark Facts and Myths" along with all the statistics he had gathered about the likelihood of running into a shark and being attacked by one.

"Surfers and fishermen get scared, too, but they know they are more likely to get struck by lightning than get killed by a shark. You're more likely to drown, more likely to get bitten by a dog, more likely to get bitten by someone on the subway in New York!" he encouraged them.

The students' eyes stayed glued to the screen. Some mouths, but no heads, dropped as Dewey presented how, over the course of one year, there were over 40,000 people injured on their toilets compared to only thirteen shark injuries.[1] Mr. Snow patted him on the back and nodded his head.

"I'm still scared though," admitted Tyler, a tall, lanky kid who always wore his skateboard logo baseball hat backwards on his head. "I know it doesn't make sense. I just am."

Once Tyler admitted it, the others confessed to feeling the same.

Each in his or her turn shared feeling afraid to go in the ocean or to take a bath at home or, in poor Ben's case, to even drink from the fountain. Dewey felt crestfallen. After all this work, had he failed?

The kids all walked out of the room seemingly grateful for his lesson.

"Great lesson, Dewey! Where'd you learn all of that stuff?"

They appreciated his information but left unaffected.

Mr. Snow just sat at his desk slowly tapping his fingers together. He seemed to be deep in thought.

"Um, thanks, Mr. Snow."

"Oh, really great job, Dewey. Thanks so much. I'll be sure you get service hours for this," he said. But he

---

1. U.S. Consumer Product Safety Commission, Washington, DC, U.S.A. (1997).
International Shark Attack File, 3 February 1998.

looked distracted, and Dewey wondered what he might be thinking.

Dewey found Seraphina and Colin sitting at the lunch tables after school, working on a poster of some sort. Seraphina had twisted her hair into a knot on top of her head. Colin sat gnawing on a pencil.

"What are you two doing?"

"Trying to come up with a slogan for our cause that unites our vending machine and t-issues. Stuck. We're stuck," Seraphina sighed.

Colin tried to talk with a big piece of banana in his mouth. "Struruck," he mumbled.

"Oh, I already have it for you," Dewey said flatly. Everything that had just occurred last period in Mr. Snow's science class still had him distracted. "'We want our Tootsie Roll—We want our Toilet Roll.' And we glue the Tootsie Rolls on the poster board along with the toilet paper."

Dewey swung his backpack over his shoulder. "See you guys in a bit," he added as he walked away.

"What?" replied Colin. "Are you kidding? That's incredible!"

"Oh boy," laughed Seraphina. "What is it with him and Tootsie Rolls?"

"Where are you going?" Colin called after Dewey.

"I gotta figure out some stuff," Dewey called back as he made his way back to his office.

1, 215 Vegetable Cookies

"1,215 vegetable cookies enough?"

Dewey came into the office Wednesday afternoon to find Clara and the office hidden behind stacks of vegetable shaped sugar cookies. Clara had stacked the cookies all over the office by their vegetable classification: leafy and salad vegetables, podded vegetables, bulb and stem vegetables, root and tuberous, and flowers and flower buds. Then, within each grouping, she made neat stacks of each of the individual vegetables into tall piles like stacks of cards. She had celery, endive, pumpkin, kale, spinach, squash, artichoke, broccoli, and carrots. On the other counter, she had one basket filled with apple cookies with a hole through the top of each. "So, you can hang them from a tree!" she explained.

Dewey stood stunned.

"Clara? What have you done? The garden isn't this big! I can't believe you did all of this in a week!"

"We're going to freeze them. That way when you start to run low, they'll be ready to go, and you can replenish right away."

"Huh!" nodded Dewey, admitting, despite the momentary utter chaos in his office, that Clara's plan made sense. He could not for the life of him figure out how she managed to make so many cookies so quickly though.

"Clara, how did you—" but before he could finish, she interrupted him.

"Boss, you've got a message here somewhere from Mr. Snow."

"Mr. Snow?" Dewey felt a small involuntary jump. "What did he say?"

"Hang on a second. I know I put it here some-where . . . I think it's under the carrots over there. No wait, hang on, maybe it's near the broccoli."

"Clara!"

"Just a minute. Oh, never mind, I know what he said. He said, 'Thanks.'"

"That's it? Just 'thanks'?"

"Yes. He said, 'Is Dewey in? Okay, well, please just tell him thanks for me.'"

"That makes no sense," Dewey said, confused. "He already thanked me. And how did he get the office number?"

"That's all I've got," replied Clara, patting herself all over and suddenly finding the message stuck in her apron pocket.

"Yes! See. Here it is. 'Thanks,'" she read and handed him the message to see for himself. "You forwarded your calls so you could get some work done. Remember?"

Dewey had forgotten, and he took the forwarding off his line. There had to be some reason Mr. Snow had gone out of his way to call, but he hadn't left a return number. Dewey would just have to be patient and wait until tomorrow. Dewey disliked being patient.

As if Clara could read his thoughts, she said, "Well, I'm sure he will let you know why when you see him, though I imagine it's probably difficult to wait."

Before leaving, Dewey told Clara about his plan for setting up the Outdoor Solar Powered Ultrasonic Animal and Pest Repeller for the office. She gave him a warm hug.

"But, sir, if it makes sounds to keep away the critters, I'm wondering if it won't bother Wolfie's ears as well?"

"Oh! I didn't think of that!" He looked online at the description and sure enough, the Outdoor Solar

Powered Ultrasonic Animal and Pest Repeller listed dogs in the description. "Whoa! Close call!" cried Dewey. "So sorry, Boy!" he said, patting Wolfie, who remained none the wiser, on his head. "I'll exchange it for this model that's just for rodents!"

"Ah, you're a peach, Boss!"

"Well, you're a plum!" They both smiled.

Dewey gave himself a small kick though. Poor Wolfie. That would have been bad. He took a deep breath as he walked out the door. Although he preferred to manage things himself, he was glad that he had Clara to help him keep his projects in order. He had a back-up system in place. Everything would be fine. He was a peach, she was a plum, Wolfie would not go mad with super-high-pitched-noises-inaudible-to-the-human-ear, and Mr. Snow was thanking him. He exhaled.

Game Time

"Anyone think it would be fun to play a game of cards or something tonight?" Dewey's dad asked. He seemed to be getting "more into the groove," as he liked to say, with his schoolwork and teaching and had more free time on his hands.

"Don. It's a school night," Dewey's mom frown.

"Um, yeah, Dad. It'd be fun, but you know, school night and all," Dewey feigned disappointment, shrugging his shoulders.

"Stephanie? Pooh B? What do you say?" That didn't seem to be stopping him.

"I say, yay!" exclaimed Pooh, eager to play a game with anyone about anything. She ran over to the hutch where they stored the games and began yanking them out onto the floor.

"Yeah, sure. I'll play for a bit," agreed Stephanie.

What? No, thought Dewey. *What just happened? This wasn't going well at all.*

"What do you say, Karen? One game?"

"Oh, okay," Dewey's mom nodded and smiled.

Dewey sighed. No escape now.

Pooh Bear walked over with her pile of games, which she reached up to put onto the table. "Which one?" she asked excitedly.

"Oh, Jenga!" cried Stephanie. "I forgot we even had that game! Let's play Jenga."

"Good, Goooood," chimed in Dewey. With Pooh playing, that should end in no time.

"Jenga it is."

"Okay. You kids going to be upset if I do the dishes? I, for one, am tired and don't want to face them later."

"Aw, Kar, I'll do them later," insisted Don.

"Nice try, Mom," teased Dewey. Dewey's mom baked bread, read to them, and hung out, but she didn't usually sit and play board games.

"I'll build the tower," said Stephanie, and she adeptly built the 54 blocks into a tall tower so they could play.

"Builder goes first." Dewey's dad gestured for her to start.

Stephanie easily slid out her first piece and placed

it on the top. Dewey's turn came next, and he had no problem doing the same. Everyone held their breath when it came to Pooh's turn.

"Okay, now, I wouldn't do that one, because—" Dewey's dad just began explaining the physics of towers to her when the whole thing came crashing down.

"Well," replied Dewey. "It's been great." He got up to go to his room. Stephanie started laughing, and Pooh, of course, burst into tears. Dewey's mom put Pooh on her lap to soothe her.

"What? No! Don't be silly, Dews! We'll start again! You're still learning, my little Padawan! Don't you know that mistakes are the BEST way to learn?"

Pooh sniffled but started to look calmer as Dewey sat back down in resignation.

"Yeah," reassured Stephanie. "I used to knock the tower down all the time when I was your age." Then she kicked Dewey under the table.

"Ouch! Hey, why'd you do that?"

She looked at him, gesturing him as if to say, *duh, your turn.*

"Oh, right, that's true. I didn't even actually start playing until I was older, Pooh." Then he added, looking at his older sister, "Okay? Geez, you didn't have to kick me that hard!"

"Sorry!" she offered. She hadn't meant to hurt him,

just wake him up. He seemed so distracted.

Dewey's dad said he and Pooh would rebuild the tower, and this time, Pooh would go first. Maybe that way, Pooh could be a scientific observer and watch and learn how they do it.

The game went on forever. Mom started to steam like a kettle left on the stove top. She wanted to blow her whistle at Dewey's dad for starting this whole thing on a school night. At ten, she gave up and went up to bed. But the rest of them couldn't figure out how to stop. Finally, at 11:45 pm, with Pooh now asleep on the couch and dirty dishes still in the sink, they agreed that if the game didn't end soon, they would call it done at midnight.

"It's 11:59, and it's . . . done. Okay, we stop," announced Stephanie sleepily. Dewey and his dad looked at one another.

"To the end?" asked Dewey.

"Loser does dishes for a week?" asked Dewey's dad.

"In!" replied Dewey.

"You guys are nuts," yawned Stephanie, picking up Pooh Bear. "I'm going to bed!"

Dewey and his dad sat there for another hour and a half. Each slowly pulling out one wooden block strategically, carefully, and then placing it on the top of the pile.

"How's school going?" asked Dewey's dad as he sat staring at the tower calculating his next move.

"Pretty good."

"Anything unexpected happen in school today?" Dewey's dad liked questions like that better than "how was school today," because he *sometimes* got something better than "I dunno," in response.

His dad slowly slid out his choice piece of wood. The tower wobbled slightly but held together as he paused and then placed it on top with a steady hand.

Dewey had already been thinking about which block he'd take next. He wondered how he might share with his dad Clara's amazing 1,215 cookies, which caught him by surprise, or the poster idea that had made his friends laugh, or any of their plans.

"I don't know," replied Dewey, and he slid out the block piece easily and put it atop the others.

"Well, do you like your classes?"

"Yeah, mostly."

"That's good. I'm finishing up my student teaching with this group, then I'll get another this semester. Too bad. I'm just finally getting to know this group."

"Yeah, it will be better when you get to keep your own class, I guess . . . Dad?" Dewey continued. "Do you have anything you're really afraid of? You know, like heights or snakes or something?"

Dewey's dad had his chosen block partially out and stopped, leaving his finger on it. "Huh," he said. "Interesting question."

Dewey couldn't believe the tower still held with the block piece part in and part out. His dad just sat there with his finger on the block, giving thought to Dewey's question.

"You know, I don't really think so. I know what you mean. My mother—Grandma—had a big fear of heights. You know, tall buildings, bridges, high heel shoes."

Dewey laughed.

"No, she wasn't really afraid of high heel shoes, but she didn't even like much to climb up the slide with me when I was young, and she made Grandpa do that."

"I get afraid at times. I can't think of one thing that I'm afraid of in that way though."

He slid out the block and flashed a smile at his success.

"You?" he asked.

"I don't think so," replied Dewey. "Not like Stephanie and spiders. I don't like them, but I don't freak out like she does."

Dewey inched out another block. He used just the tips of his fingers to grab it, and then he gently pushed it through the other side with one finger. The tower leaned precariously. The bottom level, which had begun solid, now stuck out all over the place. It stood taller than Dewey, and he had to stand on a chair now to place the next piece. It leaned far left too. Surely it would collapse soon.

"Fears are curious emotions," Dewey's dad said. He stood studying what his next move should be. "We have them for a good reason, you know. They protect us. You hear a strange thump in the dark, and you're supposed to jump. When you see a dog with foam in its mouth growling at you, your head tells your body to run—your heart beats faster, sending blood racing throughout your body so you can take off."

"I know—when Stephanie does that I always run," chuckled Dewey. "But some people get afraid when the danger is not actually there, right?" continued Dewey more seriously.

"Those are phobias, not fears. More like Stephanie with spiders, I guess. Some spiders could be dangerous, I suppose. She's more scared of the idea of spiders, but mostly they're more helpful than harmful."

"Oh, I get it. Like she's not really going to bite me, even when she growls and foams at the mouth!"

"Right!" his dad agreed with a smile. "Can we knock this thing down already?"

"Yes! Please, yes!" laughed Dewey.

"Do you want the honor?" asked Dewey's dad.

"Let's both pull out a piece," suggested Dewey.

They each pulled out a piece, and the tower crashed down. They looked at one another, afraid of getting in trouble for the loud noise they'd just made.

"Oh man, Dad, you're gonna get it."

"Fear. I feel it. Fear. And it's real."

"We'd better at least do the dishes," remarked Dewey.

"Nah, it's late. You go to bed. I got the dishes. Just put away the game for me."

"What are you going to tell Mom?"

"Son, you've got to face your fears. I'm going to tell her that I love her, and if I woke her up with that loud noise, I'm an inconsiderate lout."

"Oh," said Dewey, nodding.

"Are you kidding? I'm going to tell her I went to bed hours ago, and you kids must have made that noise."

"What?!"

"Dewey, man, back me up here."

"What? No! I don't want to get in trouble. What happened to facing your fears head on?"

"I think admitting you have fears is a good first step."

"Ugh. How about we tell her we went to bed hours ago and left the tower to show everyone in the morning, and it fell by itself?"

"GOOD! That's very good! How'd you think of that? Impressive. Frightening, really! Don't use that talent on me or your mother. Special reprieve. Mine. Not yours. Now get to bed. You're going to be tired in the morning."

Shark School

Oddly, Dewey didn't wake up feeling tired. He felt eager to know why Mr. Snow had called. Plus, he felt energized by how much work remained for them to do in the garden.

His dad had already gone to work, and his mom didn't mention last night's game at breakfast, so Dewey figured they'd gotten away with it.

As he readied to walk out the door, Dewey kissed her on the cheek and almost made a clean escape, when she chirped, "Dad told me you guys stayed up late and had fun last night. I'm glad. You'll be tired tonight. Come home early."

So he had told her after all.

"Okay," he agreed as he walked out the door.

"Wait," she called after him. "You forgot your toast." She stuck a piece of toast with avocado on it out the door after him with one hand and patted him on the head with the other. Dewey headed off to school as quickly as he could, chewing on the toast as he walked, his mind full of ideas and things to do.

When he got to school, he headed straight over to Mr. Snow's room.

"Mr. Snow?" Dewey stuck his head in the door as if somehow just one body part would be less of an interruption.

"Dewey, come in. I'll show you what I'm doing." He waved Dewey over to the page open on his computer.

"We're going snorkeling with sharks."

"What?" asked Dewey, surprised.

"Yes. I'm arranging a field trip for the students and me. Of course, you're invited. I found a place that does expeditions with leopard sharks. They are perfectly harmless, and there's no better way to get everyone over their fear than by getting up close and personal." Mr. Snow took a deep breath of air in and slowly let it out.

"Facing your fears," suggested Dewey quietly.

"Yes, gradually. We won't jump in right away, but we'll get there. I think this is going to be a good thing for all of us." Mr. Snow spoke to Dewey as he worked from his computer, arranging some of the details.

"Wow," Dewey uttered, trying to picture folks afraid of sharks swimming *with* them.

"How do you get everyone to swim with the sharks if they're so scared of them?" asked Dewey.

"Here, look at this program. They do it gradually. First the instructors are going to come in and teach us about why the leopard sharks can't harm us. They also cover why all sharks aren't something for us to fear. Then we get to go out to them, view them, and eventually touch and snorkel with them.

"So," he added, "I hope you got my message. Thanks."

"You're welcome," replied Dewey, in a reverie. It looked like he'd solved the teacher problem after all.

When he walked out to check the benches, only Seraphina had arrived.

"Hey Dewey," she greeted him, looking up from sketching in her notebook. A cold wind blew, and her hair kept whipping her face. "Catch you up?" she asked.

"Yup," he replied, sitting down beside her. "Burrr, it's cold this morning."

"I know!" she agreed. "It made me think about how we'd better get this whole thing rolled out soon before it starts to get too cold and rainy."

"Ha! Rain. We'd be lucky to get some rain around here," scoffed Dewey as they had been suffering from a drought in California for quite some time.

"Still, I think it's better not to take chances."

"Still, it's better to get our vending machine back as soon as possible!"

"True," Seraphina agreed. "Well, we're in good shape. We've got the supplies we need—more than enough cookies, that's for sure. We have the poster campaign, thanks to a certain someone . . ."

"Thank you, thank you," Dewey took a small bow, accepting credit for his part of the plan.

"The 'real garden' is going to be planted this weekend with student and parent volunteers, so I think our move must be on Sunday night. We want them to arrive to a flourishing vending machine garden Monday morning."

"Oh, that's a quick turnaround." Dewey looked up from his phone, which shouldn't have been out. The bell rang. "But I agree. Talk more at lunch. Where's Colin? He's always late! He's going to get detention!"

"Help me pack all this stuff up, would ya?"

They started to pack up her planning materials but got distracted talking again about the plans.

The second bell rang. "Ack! *We're* going to be late!" exclaimed Seraphina, gathering up her stuff. "Just go straight to the garden at lunch, and we'll finish these blueprints there."

"K," Dewey called over his shoulder as they both headed off tardy to class.

Enchantingly Late

"Miss Johnson. You seem to be running a bit late today. Have you the appropriate paperwork to excuse your dilatory arrival?" asked Mrs. Brady as she wiped her nose and slid a tissue into her sleeve. She spoke slowly and deliberately, nodding her head between each word.

"Yes, Mrs. Brady. I mean no, Mrs. Brady." Seraphina's face grew hot. "I mean, I am sorry I am late. I don't have a note."

"Thank you, Miss Johnson. Then you will find the supporting paperwork available to you in the principal's office." She turned her back to Seraphina and went back to the class.

It looked like a tardy might land on her spotless record for the first time.

"Hahaha!" she laughed aloud when she got to the line, immediately feeling better. Colin and Dewey were already waiting there to get their own readmit slips. Colin hadn't even been to class yet, and Dewey had been asked to leave class and get a readmit, as well.

"Fancy meeting you here," she greeted them. Her mom's good friend used that expression. She liked it.

Dewey laughed when he saw her. "Guess you didn't make it either."

"You know what I've never quite understood," posed Colin, "asking us to *leave* class to get us to be *in* class. Now that just makes zero sense. We are late, so they *want* to make us later?"

"I have no idea," shrugged Dewey. "Who knows why they do the things they do around here?"

They got readmits and returned to their respective classes. Seraphina entered hers feeling less embarrassed than when she had left, probably because of the time shared in line with her friends.

She handed the note to Mrs. Brady who slowly paced while reading aloud from a section of their book. Seraphina sat down, looked to Elinor sitting next to her for the page number, and found her place.

"Now I wonder who might tell me why mushrooms suddenly make an appearance right then?" Mrs. Brady asked.

No one said a word.

"Right then. How about it? Our hero has dismounted his horse, walks through the woods, and suddenly, the author sees fit to describe in detail—what?— mushrooms! Say more, someone. Kindly elucidate the author's intent."

Okay, thought Seraphina. She'd been late and lost points today. *Let's give it a go.* Up crept her hand before the rest of her arm could stop her.

"Yes, Miss Johnson?"

"Well, mushrooms are like little toadstools in the fairy world, I think. So, they can be sort of magical." Seraphina's intonation rose, beginning with "so," and peaked at the end, giving a tentative sound to her response.

Mrs. Brady closed her eyes and took a slow, long deep breath. "Ah, the world of folklore and the supernatural. Now, support this contention."

Uh oh, thought Seraphina. *I'm in too deep.* She looked again at Elinor sitting next to her for help.

"What kind of *words* might you expect to read if we're delving into something associated with fairies?" Mrs. Brady prompted. She dabbed the tip of her nose with her tissue and replaced it in her sleeve.

"They won't be found on Miss Bevel's countenance," added Mrs. Brady as Seraphina continued to look to Elinor for help.

Seraphina stared back down at the book, but everything looked like a jumble of black print.

"Miss Johnson," reiterated Mrs. Brady. "What kinds of words do you *expect* to find if we are looking for words associated with fairies as you, noted?"

"Magical?" Seraphina replied, going back to what had already worked once.

"Yes. Now, to the text. Are there any *magical* words there?"

Oh! Oh! Seraphina looked back to the text. What had been just a bunch of black and black and black on a page suddenly took on meaning. "Yes!" she exclaimed. "It says here that 'The morning mist enchanted him slowly, dropping a grey veil over his eyes.' So, that makes the mist almost like a woman who is covering his eyes so he can't see, and setting up to trick him or something. And 'enchanted' is a magical word."

"Nice, very nice," smiled Mrs. Brady warmly as she nodded and dabbed her nose with her tissue.

Seraphina relaxed in her seat and let out a sigh. She'd been so distracted lately that she hadn't been doing enough of this in class. She really did like to get answers right.

Big Sunday Planning

"I feel kind of bad," shared Seraphina later that afternoon at Colin's as they organized their Sunday night plans. "I kind of like the idea of the new garden."

"We're not destroying it," reassured Dewey. "We're just accessorizing."

"Yeah, I know," she agreed.

"Remember our motto," sang out Colin as he walked over to his closet.

"We have a motto?" laughed Seraphina.

"Yup," he replied, smiling. He'd been working overtime on his own. "We have five or six of them, actually!"

He pulled out what looked to be nothing short of fifty posters. Each poster had a Tootsie Roll glued to it, toilet paper dangling, and one of the several slogans with the words, "This Message Has Been Brought to You By the T-issue Committee and Friends of the Vending Machine."

"Oh! You mean our slogans!" said Dewey. "Let's hear them!"

"Yours first up, of course," said Colin, giving props as he unveiled the posters and slogans.

> We want Tootsie Rolls—We want Toilet Rolls
> Conservation, Not Elimination
> It's a Terrible Way to Waste
> Our Gut Tells Us This Is Wrong!
> Take the Ending Out of Vending Machines—Let
>   the Good Times Roll Again!
> Flow Freely with The T-issue Committee!

Dewey literally rolled on the floor laughing. "These are perfect!" He laughed so hard his stomach hurt. "So good! So good!"

Seraphina just shook her head. "Oh boy," she said. "Oh boy."

"I got inspired by your family's gift and just riffed off it!

"Well, that's good work, man, good work." Dewey laughed so hard his nose began to run, and he walked over and blew his nose into a tissue that dangled off the poster.

"Nooo!" yelled Seraphina and Colin together, laughing.

When they had all calmed down again, Dewey continued the planning.

"So we hang these all over the school Sunday night. We put Clara's cookies in the garden, vine the snacks, and I think we're set to go."

"Then what?" asked Seraphina.

"Then we wait," instructed Dewey.

"Wait?" she replied. "Wait for what?"

"I don't know," admitted Dewey. "Something that lets me know what to do next, I guess."

"Well, that's not much of a plan." She had assumed he had this more thought out.

"Sometimes I just have to wait to see what happens to figure out the next move. Let's just let it unfold."

Seraphina found this quite unsuitable, however. She was supposed to sneak out, hang up signs, and redesign the school garden without a next step in place?

"I don't like this," she complained. "Can't we at least think through some possibilities?"

"I think they are just going to make you nervous!"

"I'm nervous *not* thinking about them," she said.

"Well," replied Colin. "We could get arrested for trespassing."

"What?! Really?"

"Sure," replied Dewey. "Or we could get suspended for defacing property," he added.

"Geez, you guys. I just meant what our next move should be after everyone discovers the garden and the signs."

"Well, if we're not sitting on some cold stone slab of a prison cell, I guess we'll . . ." He stopped and looked at Seraphina. "I'm kidding. I'm *kidding*!" he repeated when she looked distressed.

"You go. Suggest our next move," he offered, smiling with encouragement.

"Um, we could call a meeting with the administration?"

"Sure," Dewey nodded. "We can do that."

"Yes. We can do that. Feel better?" Colin put his hand on her shoulder.

"No. We don't know what we'll say!"

"We don't know what they'll say!" Colin objected. "How can we know what we'll say?"

"Okay, okay. Just tell me the plan for Sunday," she sighed.

"Right. That, you'll be glad to know, I've got right here," and Dewey tapped the side of his head.

"Let's divide the posters up and do those first. Wolfie is coming with us to stand guard. There is no security on campus on the weekends, so it should be fine.

"Then we'll meet at the garden and set that up.

"We need to gather all the supplies for the garden and put them in a big pile in front of it. I've got the cookies. When you finish your posters, start getting the snacks you've been squirreling away. Oh, and speaking of squirrels, we need to set up the Ultrasonic Repellers. We may need to research a bit more for any other needed supplies."

"Yes, research. I like that idea. Like what?" asked Seraphina.

"Well," replied Dewey, "just picture all of our steps. Where are we putting the cookies down? In the dirt? We need something that makes sense in a garden to put them in or on to keep them safe and clean. And how are we going to hang the snacks? Fishing line? String? Hooks?"

Seraphina started to hyperventilate. "Holy cow! We're not ready at all!"

"We're really not," agreed Colin.

"And how are we even getting there?"

"I guess we just need to sneak out. Think we can do it?" asked Dewey.

"What? No way! My dad would totally notice if I snuck out of the house at night."

"My parents too!"

"Hmm. Right. Yeah, mine too," agreed Dewey. "Ha,

okay, right. New plan. We'll have to go Sunday during the day."

"DURING THE DAY?!" both Colin and Seraphina protested together.

"Yeah. It's better in some ways. Sort of. I mean, I don't think we risk jail that way," laughed Dewey. "It's much easier to just say we got confused and thought the day to do the garden work was Sunday if somebody sees us. Plus, evidently, we still have a few things to work out."

"O-kay," Seraphina replied slowly.

"Okay!" reassured Colin.

"Earlier is probably good. Let's keep it as honest as possible too. Tell our folks we're going to the school to continue some work on the garden."

"Yeah, I like that," agreed Seraphina.

"And we'll divide up the final research and supplies needed," added Dewey.

"That's good. But just how early Sunday do you have in mind? We have to get there early for the real garden, tomorrow too. I need my beauty rest, you know," drawled Colin.

"That's true. You really do," teased Dewey. "Seven Sunday morning. Can you handle that?"

"Uugh. Yeah, okay."

"Let's bring math books. If someone sees us, we'll try to say we're meeting to study math."

"Speaking of implausible . . ." laughed Colin.

"True, but it's something."

"Oh, it's something," Colin said.

"Okay, well, I'm going home to do some deep breathing with my rock collection," said Seraphina. "I'll see you both at the garden planting tomorrow. Who is looking up and bringing what for Sunday?"

"Let's see. Can you figure out how to 'plant' the cookies? I'll handle how to hang the snacks. And, Colin, you oversee how to hang the signs without defacing or damaging the paint, so we don't get in any trouble for that."

Dewey looked at Seraphina and Colin and nodded. "Okay! I'm going. If anyone gets stuck on research or supplies, text the group."

"Me, too." Seraphina walked toward the door with Dewey.

"Laters gators," said Colin, and he closed the front door.

A Snack Attack

Unlike most of the country where brown crunchy leaves began to cover the ground and the earth would soon be blanketed by snow, in southern California you could harvest a vegetable garden year-round. Beets, broccoli, Brussels sprouts, cabbage, carrots, cauliflower, chard, iceberg lettuce, onions, peas, radish, and spinach could all be planted and grown this time of year. Many of these crops were chosen to be planted this growing season in their school garden.

The Saturday garden planting had been buzzing with worker kids and parents who showed up to make sure that a healthy garden would grow at Ladera Linda Middle School.

The next morning, the sleepy garden was empty.

Neat dark rows of damp earth covered the base of young seedlings planted yesterday. A medium sized apple tree and two bird baths sat empty, awaiting the winged songbirds' arrival. Two watering cans, some trowels, and one bright pair of gardening gloves scattered about on the perimeter.

The early morning grass wet the toes of Dewey's shoes as he walked across the open field to meet his friends.

Colin already sat at the benches with the posters face down. The table had been damp, but fortunately, Colin had had the wherewithal to wipe it off before setting the posters on it.

He sat at the table and rolled up little balls of blue putty and stuck them on the back of the posters.

"Morning, Captain!"

"Good morning, Chief," replied Dewey. "Why are you using that blue stuff instead of tape?"

"This stuff sticks but doesn't damage any surface. It won't damage the walls or paint."

"Nice," said Dewey, and he joined in rolling and sticking.

"Where's all the stuff?"

"I dropped it off last night in front of the garden. Clara drove me, lugged about ten boxes."

"Isn't that kind of conspicuous?"

"Nah, I left them in the sacred vending machine spot. Between last night and now, I doubt anyone saw them."

Seraphina then showed up with two pink boxes in her hands, which could be nothing other than donuts.

"My mom wanted to bring *everyone* donuts, so here you go, *everyone*!"

"Are you serious? Two dozen donuts for the three of us. That's a good ratio," grinned Colin, picking out one sprinkled and one glazed and taking a two-fisted bite of each.

"Just don't get any jelly on the signs," cautioned Dewey.

"Eww, jelly? No, I didn't get any jelly," reassured Seraphina, tilting the box to show him. "My feet are all wet from that grass. There's a lot of dew when you get here this early." She grabbed a donut napkin to wipe her toes.

"Hey, dew. Get it? Dew. Dewey. You're Dewey!"

"Is that the first time you've ever thought of that?" asked Dewey.

"Yes, I think it is." She grabbed a donut and set it down on a napkin, licking her fingers before wiping them on her pants.

"Did your parents name you for the morning dew? That's so poetic!" She pinched off some blue putty to roll and stick on the back of the posters.

"Yeah, Dewey. Very poetic," chuckled Colin.

"No. After some famous guy whose last name was Dewey."

"Oh yeah, who?" asked Seraphina, pulling out her phone and preparing to look it up.

"Can we maybe do this later?" suggested Dewey. "It's getting late."

"Yeah," joked Colin. "Let's *Dewey* this later."

Dewey rolled his eyes.

"Okay, okay," conceded Seraphina. "But you know I love that stuff."

The posters all had the putty on them and stuck to one another because there were so many of them, they'd had to stack them up. They would each have to carefully peel their own stack apart as they hung them.

"You know what to do. I got the south part of campus. Colin, go east and west. Seraphina, you go north."

"And what do we do again if someone sees us?" asked Seraphina.

"Yeah? Hey, where's Wolfie?" asked Colin.

"I decided it would be harder to explain being here with a dog. Besides, he can't guard three places at once."

"Hmm. Maybe," shrugged Seraphina.

"Don't open any locked doors," cautioned Colin.

"That's the stupidest suggestion I've ever heard,"

laughed Dewey. "How are we going to open them if they are locked?"

"Hmm. Well, don't go into any offices or anything."

"We're not complete noobs," Seraphina reassured. "We're just hanging these in major corridors and hangout spots."

"Okay, okay. Everybody relax. We got this. Operation We want Tootsie Rolls—We want Toilet Rolls, commence action!"

They all just stood there.

"Okay, great for a poster—not so excellent for moving troops," Colin said, shaking his head.

Dewey laughed. "Okay, then. Go!"

The three of them went separate directions.

As he went east, Colin could hear his footsteps walking down the usually busy corridors. The morning air still felt cool against his skin as he carried his signs.

He set them down in a pile on the ground and picked his first spot for hanging a sign. He decided over the water fountain would be good and pressed the four corners of "Conservation, not Elimination" onto the wall.

He pressed the edges down on the top two corners and then the bottom two, rubbing carefully as he did so. Then, for extra measure, he used his fist as a hammer.

Next, he grabbed "T-ISSUE: It's a Terrible Way to

Waste" and hung that right in front of his math teacher's classroom.

Colin papered the walls down the hallway and then the areas over the lockers as well. He then headed to the west part of campus where the cafeteria and the nurse's office were locked. He wouldn't have gone in the nurse's office, but the cafeteria would have been cool. Instead, he hung signs outside the bathroom doors because they fit so perfectly with their campaign.

The top of his arms tired. His heart jumped when he heard a noise. He froze expecting to look up to see someone there, but all remained quiet and empty as Colin hung his signs. He must have imagined it.

Colin's mind wandered as he worked some more. He should have brought his drone with him today. It would have been so great to fly it on the soccer field. You're not allowed to do that at school, of course, but with no one around, it would have been perfect.

How could he manage to go back and get it now? He probably couldn't.

Thirty minutes later, the team met back at the garden, each with nothing extraordinary to report other than that their mission had been accomplished.

"It's quiet around here," observed Seraphina.

"No, no, no. Now you've done it!" cried Colin. "Quick. Go knock on some wood, three times!"

"What? Why?" asked Seraphina.

"You're gonna jinx us," he warned, getting up and looking around until he found something he thought would satisfactorily ward of the evil she'd invited and knocked three times.

"Where does that come from, anyway?" asked Dewey.

"My mom!" replied Colin.

"No, I mean originally. Why do people knock on wood? Didn't you say your grandmother used to spit three times?"

"Ha! Yes," laughed Seraphina. "But could we puh-leez get back to work?"

"Yeah, sure. You and Dewey are the ones getting us off track!" scolded Colin.

"Puh-leez," Seraphina reiterated.

Dewey laughed, "You're a nut, Colin." He then redirected them to the boxes under the overhang where the vending machines used to sit.

"There's a lot of stuff. We'd better get going."

"How are we hanging the snacks?" Seraphina asked.

"Fishing wire, ribbons, string," Dewey replied, lifting the lid on one of the boxes.

"Okay, well, let's move some earth, Worms! Get it? Earthworms? Move some—get it?"

Dewey did a whole body shudder. "Worms. Gross."

Colin laughed.

"I love worms! They feel all slimy and smooth as they inch along," Seraphina said.

"Like a wet booger," Dewey shuddered again, and his friends laughed.

They each stacked a few boxes and headed into the garden.

Seraphina had researched landscape fabrics to put the cookies atop and had strips of fabric to lay in the garden. "Try not to put them where the real seeds are so we don't mess them up," cautioned Dewey.

"Oh, I know just how to do it." Seraphina held up some fabric for Dewey to inspect. "I got the woven kind. If I put it in the right spots, the material will protect the real plants better by helping the soil keep its moisture. Win-win, baby!" She began to lay down the strips and set out rows of plant cookies.

As Seraphina planted the cookies, Colin began hanging chips, nuts, snack bars, and jerky from the green pea trellises. Dewey supplied lines of thin fishing wire and a hole puncher, and Colin tied the line through the holes. Dewey picked the bird fountain as the most fitting place to nest the beverages. Their vending machine didn't have sodas, and they would never win a battle to get colas at middle school. So just bringing back the cold beverages they did allow would have to do. He loaded up the bird bath with drinks like it was a cooler at a picnic, and then moved to stringing the apple cookies to hang in the tree.

They had forgotten to bring a step stool or ladder, but Dewey found one of Shawn's leaning up against the wall outside of the gym. Both Seraphina and Colin held the ladder when Dewey climbed it to hang the apples. That became a three-person job because they knew that if any one of them broke an arm, the whole mission would be compromised.

They worked three and a half hours straight. The sun warmed up the garden as the day grew, but it still felt cool out. Colin's appetite also began to grow, and he threatened to eat the display.

"Well, I'm starving!" he said, hanging up his last bag of mini pretzels. "A man cannot live on eighteen donuts, you know."

"Whoa," whispered Dewey as he stepped back to look at what they'd done. "Whoa."

Neat tidy rows of celery, endive, pumpkin, kale, spinach, squash, artichoke, broccoli, and carrot cookies lined the garden. Bags of chips, pretzels, cookies, candy, granola bars, corn nuts, crackers, trail mix, Pop-Tarts, beef jerky, and popcorn hung from the pea cages and trellises like colorful mobiles—merry-go-rounds of snacks. Red and green iced apple cookies with little green and brown stems dangled from above. Before them stood a three-dimensional vending machine wonderland—a garden of snacks.

"Look, you guys. Look."

They brushed the dirt off from their hands and knees, and the pair stood back with Dewey.

"Holy narwhal!"

"Wow. We did all of this? I'm pretty impressed with us!"

"The last thing to do is add the repellers." Dewey pulled two of them out of the last box.

"We probably only need one, but I got two just to be safe," he said.

"You got batteries for them, right Dewey?" asked Seraphina, worried. "Dewey? Right?"

Dewey stood dead still. Batteries. "Ugh. No. No!"

Colin took one out of the box and fiddled with the battery compartment to open it up.

"Colin, it says right here on the box, 'requires four lithium metal batteries.'"

"They're here!"

"Let me see!" Dewey raised his arms high over his head. "Clara! The best assistant EVER!"

They set up the two pest repellers at either end of the garden.

Then they all stood rapt and still.

Dewey broke the silence. "Well, I'd say our work

here is done. Or just begun. Or something. But we should go get a big burger and see where all of this takes us tomorrow!"

"Where all of us takes this," Seraphina, almost in a trance, jumbled Dewey's words.

"Help me pack up this box, and let's get out of here. I can hardly wait until tomorrow."

"Until tomorrow, I can hardly wait." Seraphina did it again.

The Big Dewey

Dewey's mom sat in her fuzzy pink robe sipping on iced coffee and pointed to a bowl of oatmeal she had made for him. She usually wore contact lenses, but she had glasses on this morning. She pulled her messy morning hair back in a ponytail. *This has the potential to be a nice moment,* she thought. No Pooh Bear or Stephanie meant maybe they would have a quiet couple of minutes to themselves. It had been a while.

"Dewey? We should do something this weekend."

"Sure, Mom. Okay. What do you want to do?" Dewey took a bite of his oatmeal which tasted thick and cold, as usual, because he never came down to breakfast soon enough.

"Anything you like. What sounds fun to you?"

Dewey couldn't concentrate on this conversation. His thoughts drifted to school and how teachers and administrators would start arriving soon and see their signs and the garden.

"Dews?" his mom prompted again.

"Huh?"

"This weekend?"

"Oh, I don't know. Whatever you want, Mom."

"Whatever I want? Well, that's great! Let's go to the botanical gardens."

"I hate the botanical gardens," replied Dewey, plopping his porridge back in his bowl.

"Are you going to eat that or just build a sand sculpture?"

"A sand sculpture?"

"Dewey, eat your breakfast."

Dewey's mom had hoped for more pleasant breakfast talk.

"Dewey."

"Huh?"

"Do you have something on your mind, son?"

"Not really," and Dewey scooped up a big spoonful of oatmeal and took a bite. "Mom? Who is the Dewey you named me after, again?"

"John Dewey!"

"But who was he?"

"Oh, probably the greatest educational thinker of his era!"

"So he was a teacher?"

"Yes, he was a teacher. But he was also a philosopher and an educational reformer."

"And you guys like him."

"We guys *love* him! You know, your dad and I love the idea of education and social reform. Go out and change the world; education to transform. It's why really, in his heart, your dad has always wanted to teach, and why I still would love to open a school one day."

Open a school? This was news to Dewey. He knew his mom used to teach before he was born. Now she spent her time—well, he had no idea what she did with her time.

Anyway, this was all very nice, but he wasn't expecting such a long answer right now and felt sorry he'd gotten her started.

"Hey, Google," Dewey called out. "What time is it?"

"The time is 7:20 am," reported the robotic assistant.

"Oh, I gotta go! I need to brush my teeth still."

"Go!" she encouraged. "I got it," she added to indicate she'd clear his place for him.

He gave her a warm smile.

The Big Day

Dewey arrived at school right on time. He wondered what he would find.

Just yesterday, Dewey and his friends could hear only the sound of their own breath and footsteps. Now, the corridors stirred with a cloudy brew of voices and laughter. The wide empty hallways gave way to moving legs and swinging arms. As Dewey got closer to the heart of their handiwork, the movement and air around him shifted.

Here, matchstick legs with rolled down socks, blue jeans, and a scattering of Crayola colored tights stood still. The air hung with anticipation. Dewey and the others expected the garden to generate a big buzz. Instead, the silence of wonder and awe greeted them.

"Whoa," whispered Colin to Dewey when they found one another. "Maybe they haven't seen the signs yet?"

"Still." remarked Dewey, who had expected a rush for the garden goods and a lot of laughter at their signs.

"Let's go where some signs are and see what's going on there."

They found kids gathered around their signs talking to one another.

"Yeah, I agree," said seventh grader Lukas. "Why are we suffering under these conditions?" The only thing Dewey really knew about Lukas was that masking tape with the words "chicken nugget" held his glasses together.

"How come they took away our vending machine, actually? They never talked to us about it. We should tell the student government to have a meeting. Do we have a student government?" Ava asked.

"Of course we do," Paloma said. "Who do you think plans the dances?"

Seraphina approached Colin and Dewey. "We definitely caused a stir," she whispered. "Students all over campus aren't going to class. I think the administration is going to call an all-school meeting."

Dewey's eyes got big. He could feel an "okay, what's next?" coming on. He stood there really hoping she didn't ask that question.

"Okay, then. So . . . what's next?"

"Well, I think we have backers now. We should be ready to make a case at that meeting."

"Make a case saying what?" asked Colin.

"You gotta show them we can conserve paper in some other way. And Seraphina and I should prove that they don't have to take our vending machine for us to have a garden. Somehow. We gotta do our research."

"Research? Meeting? We need more time!" wailed Seraphina. "We don't even know what we're going to say!"

"Okay, you go ask Mrs. Mayoral if we can have the meeting tomorrow, not today. Tell them a bunch of students are asking for more time to get ready before the meeting, so she doesn't think it's just us."

"What? No! Why me?"

"Okay. We'll rock, paper, scissor it. Colin, let's go."

The first time, they all did rock. The second time, Dewey guessed they'd all do rock again, so he did paper instead, and he and Seraphina both lost to Colin.

Seraphina and Dewey now went up against one another. "Rock, paper, scissors."

"Rock," the both called out in unison.

"Rock, paper, scissors."

"Paper," again in unison. They both laughed.

"Rock, paper, scissors." This time Dewey lost, his paper to Seraphina's scissors.

"Fine," huffed Dewey. "I'll do it."

"I was going to make you do it anyway. It was your bright idea to 'just let it unfold.'"

The bell rang to go to class though, and Dewey was saved by the announcement over the loudspeaker that told the students there would be a school-wide assembly tomorrow morning to discuss the recent activities and developments. No one went to class. More and more students gathered around the garden to stare at its temptation, but no one dared enter it.

"I think we need to get them started," suggested Colin, and he walked in, took a carrot cookie, and began to munch.

"Yeah!" Moses walked into the garden. "Isn't that what the administration said? We're supposed to harvest our snacks?" He grabbed a bag of chips off a vine and tossed it to Amelia who laughed eagerly.

Colin, Dewey, and Seraphina looked to one another. Now the other kids caught on. Before long, the garden hopped and buzzed with kids feeding on the bounty that the three of them had sown.

"Careful not to step on the other seedlings," cautioned Paloma as she bent down herself to harvest some "broccoli."

"It's easy not to. It's all laid out perfectly. It's brilliant!" cried Moses, stuffing a "bell pepper" into his mouth and opening a bag of chips.

Dewey, Seraphina, and Colin smiled.

That night, each of the three vending machine gardeners sat busy, digging for information to help their cause. You'd think Seraphina, who'd been researching, collecting, cleaning, labeling, trimming, and displaying her rock collection for the past five years, would be the best at it. She had field notebooks filled with words like diaphany, but when she sat down at the computer and entered a search for "Ladera Linda" and "vending machines," all she could feel was her throat tighten and a growing desire to throw something across her room.

"Just come over here," proposed Dewey.

So Seraphina and Dewey worked together at Dewey's house.

"According to what it says here, the school district is participating in some U.S. Department of Agriculture program, 'Smart Snacks in Schools.' It has a lot of rules about what the snacks should be like. That's got to be part of what's going on." Seraphina began.

"It says snacks should be 'less than or equal to 200 calories, 200 mg of sodium, and with total fat and sugar less than—'"

"Or equal to?" interrupted Dewey, smiling. "Do you know what I just heard you say? I got, blah, blah 200, blah blah, 200, less than or equal to, blah, blah, blah."

"Yes," Seraphina continued, ". . . with a total fat and sugar of less than 35% of calories. Per serving."

"Exactly. Blah, blah blah, blah, blah, 35%, blah."

Meanwhile, Colin began his search setting out to prove that rigging the toilet paper rolls didn't save paper. His findings, though, were proving otherwise.

"What?!" he called out to no one when he discovered that the Cloud Nine paper mills alone produced enough tissue to wrap around the Earth's circumference 1 $^1/_2$ times—every day! *EVERY DAY!*

Colin Facetimed, and Dewey propped up his phone so everyone could see each other. "Hang on, Colin. Just in the middle of a thought here."

"Ha!" laughed Seraphina. "Nice to know you're thinking between the blahs."

"Hmm," continued Dewey. "Let's apply it. Potato chips."

Seraphina typed them into her search.

"Mmm. Potato chips," hummed Colin. "I'll be right back," and he headed off to the kitchen to forage for a salty snack.

"Let's see," reported Seraphina. "160 Calories, 90 from fat . . ."

"Oh, that's not bad! What percent is it?"

"Um . . . 16%!"

"What about the salt? The sodium?".

"170 mg!"

"Hey! I think the Wellness Committee can list Potato Chips on their 'Smart Snacks' document. Excellent. What else? Let's try something else. You pick it and I'll search."

CRUNCH. CRUNCH. CRUNCH.

"Colin! Are you doing *any* work over there?" demanded Dewey.

"A man," CRUNCH CRUNCH, "must fortify himself," CRUNCH CRUNCH, "to think."

"Just hang up," Seraphina implored. "I can't concentrate."

"We'll call you back." Dewey hung up.

"Okay," she said. "How about Twix Bars?"

"250 calories. Out. Give me another."

"Snickers?"

"Nope. 250. I think candy bars are out. We never had much candy in our vending machine anyway. Why are you looking at candy? Try cookies."

"Oh! Chips Ahoy. Those are good."

"That's better," Dewey approved nodding his head slowly as he read. "Calories 160, total fat 11%, sugar is 11 grams. Hmm. They don't say what percent that is of the calories. Now *we* need to do some math," Dewey stared at Seraphina, waiting for her to be the "we" in that equation.

"Haha! Okay. Move over. Let's see. If the sugar is 11 grams, and the—"

Dewey's phone rang. Colin was Facetiming them again.

"Oh, no. Oh no, oh no, oh no, oh no."

His face disappeared from the screen.

"Colin? Where'd you go?" Dewey held up the phone to show Seraphina the screen, which showed Colin's room, but no Colin.

"I can't find it. I'm dead. I'm dead meat. My dad's gonna kill me."

"What?" Seraphina asked. "Colin, what's going on?"

"I can't find my retainer. Seriously. My dad is going to go berserk. I already lost one. I can't lose this one."

"Well, when d—" Dewey interrupted himself. "Colin! Come back to the phone. I can't talk to you this way. Where are you?"

"Under the bed."

"Why would your retainer be under the bed?"

"I don't know. I don't know. I don't know. I don't know."

"Colin, come out, sit on the bed, and talk to us."

Colin's frantic face appeared on the screen.

"When did you have it last?" Seraphina asked

"I took it out to eat the chips," recalled Colin, nodding slowly. "I think. Oh, I don't know."

Dewey muted the phone. "This is no good. We're never going to get anything done, and he's not going to finish his research! I'm going over there to help him find it."

"What? Now? And leave me with all of the work?" objected Seraphina the tight feeling returning to her throat.

Colin could be heard talking to them in the background, but they were missing his words as they spoke.

"Okay, then come with me," suggested Dewey, throwing up his arms.

He unmuted the phone.

"Uh huh," he replied as if he'd been listening all along. "We're coming over. We'll find it. Calm down, though, would ya?"

"Where'd he go?" Seraphina asked. Colin had left the screen again.

"Who knows?" shrugged Dewey. "This is going to be a long night."

Retainer Container

They parked their bikes in Colin's carport and headed up to his apartment. Colin's dad didn't appear home yet as his car wasn't in his spot.

When they knocked on the door, Colin opened it and both Seraphina and Dewey laughed. His hair, usually a loose mass of thick black spirals and curls a good three inches around his head, now looked frazzled.

"What happened to your hair?" asked Dewey kindly as he put his hand on his shoulder.

"What? My hair? I don't know," answered Colin, but it soon became clear as he repeatedly raked his fingers through it, pacing the room, and mumbling his dead meat mantra.

"When is your dad coming home?" asked Seraphina.

"What? He's home. He's in his office doing some work."

"Oh, I didn't see his car."

"Shop. In the shop."

"Okay, let's go to your room," suggested Dewey.

When they got upstairs, Dewey forced Colin to sit down while he and Seraphina did a check around the room. No retainer.

"I'm going to check online for ideas."

"Online?!" scoffed Colin. "You can't just go, 'Hey Siri, where is my retainer?'"

"Calm down," said Seraphina. "You aren't the first one to lose a retainer."

"I'm the second one, if you count me."

"Huh?" asked Dewey confused.

"It's the second one I've lost!" clarified Colin. "Oh, man, he's gonna kill me!"

"Ha! Here! 'How to Find your Retainer,' on WikiHow! We'll just follow the steps."

"This is dumb," objected Colin, but he let out a big sigh.

"We don't really have a better plan, Colin. And we have a school meeting tomorrow, which we *have* to get back to preparing for, so let's just give this a try, okay?"

"Yeah, yeah, okay." Colin paced his room, looking for his retainer under every book and sweatshirt. In his next move, Colin began to madly empty out his closet.

"Colin!" called out Dewey.

"Huh?" he stopped his digging.

Dewey walked Colin over to the edge of his bed and sat him down.

Seraphina continued reading:

"'*Step 1: Stay calm. Otherwise, your stress hormone level will rise, causing you to have a fast pulse and sweaty palms. These intense emotions cloud your judgment and memory, can easily distract you from being able to recall where you last had it.*'"

Dewey picked up Colin's wrist and tried to take his pulse.

"Knock it off," laughed Colin, slapping away Dewey's hand.

"Step 2 is to '*look everywhere.*'"

"I've done that!" wailed Colin.

"No, we have to do it 'systematically, not'—haha! It's like they're watching you, Colin—'*throwing items around and digging through things in a panic.*'" Seraphina and Dewey laughed.

"Not funny," growled Colin.

"It says to approach each room like a crime scene. We work in each room you've been in, cover each area of space, and work in concentric circles. Oh, and it says to do it in levels." Seraphina clapped her hands together.

"This is going to be fun!" she said. "Should we split up areas or share the space in a room and each cover one area within it?"

"I don't know," sulked Colin. He took a nosedive into his bed pillows like his drone crash landing.

"Let's do it together," encouraged Dewey. "We'll start in here, cover the kitchen, and then the stairway. Any other rooms you were in? Think hard, Colin."

"No, I think that's it," he lifted his face from the pillows long enough to reply. "But what are we telling my dad if he sees us?"

"Science project. It's my standard reply. Always works. They always want to know more about it. Just look like you're concentrating really hard adding numbers up, and they'll leave you alone."

"Okay. Let's start in here then," said Seraphina dragging Colin back up.

They covered every inch of Colin's room, the stairs, and the kitchen. Colin's dad did come in and say hello, but he never questioned them. He did, however, wonder if they wanted some dinner. Dewey and Seraphina both called home to ask if they could do a project at Colin's and eat pizza there, which thankfully got the go-ahead. They would have to leave their bikes and get a ride home though, since it would get dark.

After over an hour of solid searching, and a pizza

break where Colin faked taking out his retainer so his dad wouldn't notice, they headed back up to Colin's room defeated.

"I really think we need to work on the t-issue and the garden presentation some more. You're just going to have to tell your dad or hope it shows up," said Dewey.

Dewey sat down at the computer and began to go back to the research on snack food and the vending machines.

"No. Nuh uh. Nope." Colin folded his arms over his chest and stood staring at the wall.

"Move out of my way," said Seraphina to Dewey, and she switched Dewey's page and resumed reading from the WikiHow list.

"'*Step 3: Sit down—*'"

At this, Dewey stood up and put both hands on Colin's shoulders and pressed him down on the bed.

"'*—and think about what you were doing the last time you remember having it.*'"

"Okay. Let's see . . ."

"No, wait," interrupted Seraphina, putting up her pointer finger. "There's more. Listen to what it says first. For step 4, they want us to recreate the whole scene. What you were feeling, doing, the flavors of the chips, and what you did next. We are supposed to recreate the whole thing."

"I can't. I'm too stressed," he cried, and he ran his fingers through his hair again, dragging the life out of any hopeful curls.

"Okay, let me just see what else is left do, and then we'll recreate the scene. Hmm. Oh, look! You already did step 5! Good job! *'Get Help. If all else fails, ask someone to help you search. Other people won't feel the same anxiety you might be feeling, so they can search with a clear head,'*" read Seraphina.

"No. Not true," interjected Dewey. "I'm anxious. No clear head. I'm getting stressed. Str-essed!"

"Okay," began Seraphina, ignoring Dewey. "You were on the phone with us, and you got hungry. You wanted chips, put the phone down, and went to get them. Do you think you had your retainer then? How were you *feeling?*"

"Hungry," answered Colin.

"And where did you go? What did you do? What kind of chips were they? Tell us more."

"Yeah, Colin, tell us more," poked Dewey, trying to join in and relax but his words came out a bit more sarcastic than he'd intended.

"Not helpful," replied Seraphina.

"I was researching the history of toilet paper. I called you guys. You guys started talking about potato chips. That made me in the mood for some. I went to the kitchen, hoping we had some. We had a bag of Takis Fuegos. I grabbed the bag and ate them."

"Not so fast," replied Dewey, trying to be more helpful. "Where did you open them? You ate them with us on the phone to start? Or downstairs?"

"I tried to open them in the kitchen, but I couldn't get the bag open until halfway up the stairs. I opened the bag with my teeth, so I pu—"

Colin jumped up, reached into his pocket, and took out his retainer.

"Oh."

He plopped back down on his bed with a big sigh, and slipped his retainer back in his mouth.

Seraphina and Dewey each plopped down on the bed.

"'*Step 6: Order a retainer container.*'"

A Different Approach (Duh)

They spent the rest of the evening working on the presentations for the morning meeting at school.

Colin redeemed himself by finding a "Smart Snacks Product Calculator," which quickly told them if the snacks met the criteria or not, simply by entering the item, which saved a lot of time. He worked on his laptop on his bed, while Dewey and Seraphina worked at his desk.

"Throw in some whole-grain Sun Chips, and I think we've rebuilt the vending machine with what even our own Department of Agriculture would call—Dewey. No, wait. No, no, Dewey. I think we read this wrong," Seraphina's eyes darted across the screen.

"What do you mean?" Dewey felt his face get hot

with panic again. He thought they had almost finished. They still needed to go home and organize their findings into a presentation. His whole body ached with exhaustion.

"The requirements say 'also.' See? 'Foods must *also* meet several nutritional requirements.'"

"What else do they want?"

"Um, they want the first ingredient to be a fruit, vegetable, dairy, or protein."

"Ugh, Pop-Tarts won't work. But the potato chips still do! Right? Potatoes are a vegetable, right? Right? RIGHT?!"

"Yes, I think so," Seraphina nodded and started to look it up.

"Here, let me sit down."

"Wait. Let me just see first. Okay, yes. They are botanically considered vegetables."

"Good! Okay, so move over," he said sliding his bottom into her seat. "Let's see. Put it in the calculator. It's looking good. Sugar is less than 1%. Fat is low, I think? 10 grams which is just 16%. They have 10% potassium. That's got to be a good thing."

"Do they work?" she asked, holding her breath.

"Hang on . . . No! The calories from fat exceeds 35%! Oh, this is terrible." Dewey slumped down in Colin's desk chair.

"I don't think apples and green bean casserole in the vending machines are going to be all that popular," she rolled her eyes.

"I'm good with apples. I like the apples. Save the apples!"

"Dewey, you're getting preposterous."

"I'm getting overtired," he moaned.

"Move." With her bottom, Seraphina shoved Dewey out of the seat again so she could sit at the computer. She sat up tall. "Okay, so the snacks in the vending machine are clearly not going to cut the mustard," she said.

"Ha! Mustard! Mustard is not a food group," Dewey bounced back.

"Colin? How you doing?"

"I can't believe it, but toilet paper waste is a HUGE problem. We use like fifty-seven sheets a day which they say adds up to about fifty pounds a year. I can see why they're trying to get us to stop using so much."

"So you want to give up the t-issue?" asked Dewey.

"No, I can't do my business at school with one little sheet at a time. I just sit there forever pulling off sheets, anyway. I'm not saving paper, I'm wasting time."

"We need to figure out how to get *that* message across," said Dewey.

"Right," Seraphina nodded. "I think that's the right thinking."

"Why does *my* business have to be *everyone's*?" Colin objected.

"You don't have to share the primary source details! We just have to get them to understand that their attempt to save paper probably isn't working the way they planned."

"What do you think the expression 'doesn't cut the mustard' means?" asked Dewey.

"Huh?" asked Colin.

"I know it means that something isn't good enough, but why do they say 'cut the mustard'? How can you cut mustard?"

"Why are we talking about this?" inquired Colin.

"I better ask my mom if I can stay here and work more," Seraphina suddenly remembered.

"Ugh. Me too," Dewey checked the time on his phone.

They still had a lot of work to do. Seraphina's mom agreed to pick her up at 8:30 and give Dewey a ride home. They grabbed slices of cold pizza and kept working.

Hours after Seraphina and Dewey had left, Colin texted them a link showing that he'd put mustard into the Smart Snacks Product Calculator. "Mustard doesn't cut the mustard," he joked.

No matter how they worked it, the bottom line seemed to be that the committee had it rigged to make their snacks all fail.

It was now well after ten, and they Facetimed from their respective bedrooms.

"I'm so tired," groaned Seraphina. "This isn't working. We need a different approach."

"Maybe we should all just be working together again and doing it the same way."

"Yeah," chuckled Dewey. "Toilet paper in the vending machines and Pop-Tarts in the bathrooms."

"No," continued Colin, yawning as he spoke. "I mean they," another yawn, "don't know what they're doing. They want to save paper for the right reasons, but they're doing it all," yawn "wrong."

"And?" Seraphina asked.

"And they want us to eat healthy, but they're doing that wrong too. 'Smart Snacks,' my asparagus!"

Dewey and Seraphina laughed, perking up a bit.

"They didn't even talk to us, they just snip our toilet paper rolls and swipe our vending machines. We can still eat junk if we bring it from home, right?" said Dewey.

"It's a crime to deny us our royal rolls and Tootsie Rolls! We'll approach it like a crime scene!" laughed Colin. "Let's use the WikiHow steps we used to find my retainer. Room by room, problem by problem. You know, in levels."

Dewey and Seraphina laughed again. Colin had begun to rant.

"Well, I'm just saying."

"Yes!" nodded Seraphina with enthusiasm. "We just need to approach it from the ground up."

"Now, you're doing something to help us!" ribbed Dewey. But it made sense, and he felt grateful for some solid thinking right about now.

"Alright, then. Step 1 again. We stay calm. Then we can do the levels and concentric circles. Breathe and cover each of our bases," Seraphina instructed.

Seraphina started looking around more online and found proof that denying kids sweets actually causes them to pig out more.

"It's true. Whenever Aiden comes over, he's on the chips and cookies like a fly on garbage," laughed Dewey. "I don't think his parents ever let him have any."

"Well, I'm finding good data we can use!" Seraphina had the keyboard in her lap, and her feet back up on the desk as she worked.

She also found a couple of articles that talked about how involving students in decision-making led to much better results.

"Oh! This is going to work!" she let out a big sigh

and pulled the scrunchy out of her hair, letting her long brown hair tumble down.

Colin found what he needed to prove it was better to show kids how to use toilet paper properly and economically, rather than using that gizmo. They all jumped up and down. Colin's dad came up to come up to see if they'd "let in a herd of elephants."

Then they had their biggest breakthrough.

Dewey read on the toaster pastry site, wishfully thinking that the strawberry ones might have real strawberries as their first ingredient, when he discovered a golden nugget: *"Hey, kids! Did you know your tasty toaster pastries just got more tops? We've added ¹/₂ a serving of whole grain. Talk about toasty fiber!"*

"No way!" said Dewey. "That can't be a coincidence. I think they're making special ones that work for the Smart Snack Rules!"

"I'll bet you're right. What about the other snacks?"

It was true. All their favorite kind of snacks had versions with lower sodium, lower sugar, and lower calories from fat.

"Whoa! That's amazing," said Dewey.

"I'll tell you what that is," croaked Colin, his voice sleepy but his mind now wide awake. "That's big business using us kids as pawns. They want to sell us their goods, so the government tries to stop them, and then they just, just, mutate it to meet the new standards.

"It's an outrage. I, for one, am outraged!" He put up his pointer finger in outrage, but just a little tardily, as his sleepy arm didn't quite keep pace with his passionate mouth.

Seraphina laughed. "I don't disagree. But it's pretty hilarious to hear you getting yourself in a dither over Ding Dongs! You're not exactly opposed to eating that kind of stuff."

"I'm not. I just don't like everyone telling us what to do. It's what my dad always says—"

"You have to laugh at your own jokes because if you don't no one else is going to?" laughed Dewey.

"That's not how it goes. And no. 'Everything in moderation.'"

"That's true. I agree with that. Clara has baked probably like 4,000 cookies for us over the years. Colin's only eaten half of them. They should give us some credit. Have some faith!"

"No wonder they got rid of the vending machines. Between these crazy standards and the fact that, even after you do follow them, you still end up with a bunch of junk, they can't figure out how to regulate it," Seraphina said pointing to the computer screen.

"Right," said Dewey. "Obviously, we need to learn to control ourselves. There won't always be little gizmos parceling out the toilet paper of life!"

"Oh, that's beautiful, Dewey," Colin nodded, sniffing and wiping a pretend tear.

Seraphina laughed.

"Okay," said Dewey. "That's our presentation! Healthy choices. Some grub food. Toilet paper that rolls. Teach us to make good decisions. Don't roll too much. Don't eat too much. Don't lie, don't cheat, don't steal. Water your garden, and viva Las Vegas."

They stayed up most of the night gathering their data and getting ready for the meeting.

At four in the morning, they finally went to sleep. With three hours bolstering their heavy eyelids, they headed off to school feeling ready for what was ahead.

Farmer Bacon Speaks

Principal Mayoral stood no taller than most of her students. In fact, a good many of them had gained a solid inch or three over her since the summer. What she didn't have in height, she made up for in eloquence and stature. A room full of children settled down for her without incident. Was it her eyes that told them she cared too much about their well-being and their learning to let them misbehave? Or the swift consequences she doled out when they did? Principal Mayoral wore her hair close-cut, with tight grey curls. Her closed-toe navy shoes with square heels stood firmly planted before them in the gymnasium where the entire school assembled. She began her address by citing California's Vandalism Law, Penal Code 594. "California's vandalism law," she read ominously, "prohibits doing any of the following things to school or other property: maliciously defacing it with graffiti, damaging it, or destroying it."

Colin, Seraphina, and Dewey sat near one another, but none dared to look at the others.

"Vandalism?" considered Dewey. A fascinating and disturbing development.

"Are they going to arrest us?!" Seraphina fretted to herself as she tried to quietly take deep breaths.

"Oh, oh," Colin said quietly.

"Vandalism, as you know," continued their principal, "is a serious offense. And yet, we find ourselves in a bit of a quandary. Do broccoli cookies constitute damage? Are Tootsie Roll signs graffiti? Are dangling Doritos and tethered Twix malicious acts?

"We do not approve of students on campus, without adult supervision, outside of school hours. But we would like to hear from the student body now what the student grievances are. Clearly, you all have some concerns on your minds.

"At this time, we will turn over the microphone to students to bring up any questions, concerns, or suggestions they have about vending machines, restroom conditions, or anything else that impacts student lives here at school, which may not have made it on the walls or into the halls of our campus but may still need addressing.

"Students of Ladera Linda, you have our attention."

She sat down and turned the microphone over to the student body president, Julia Jack.

"Is there someone who would like to come speak first?"

Dewey looked at Colin, who looked at Seraphina, who looked at Dewey.

"Oh great," Dewey whispered to them. "Colin is a much better crowd guy. You go first."

"Okay," Colin agreed, and his hand shot up.

So did Ben's, one of the boys who'd been fearful of the water fountain in Mr. Snow's class.

"Ben," called Julia, motioning him up.

"Yes. I'd just like to take this time to say that I liked the vending machines a lot, and I would like them back."

Then he just stood there.

"Is that it?" Julia asked.

Ben nodded.

"Okay, thanks," she said.

Colin's hand shot up again, and she nodded for him to come up.

"Lights, please," Colin requested after he set up his Google Slides. He began to share the history of toilet paper.

"As long as there have been humans, there have been people peeing and pooping," he began.

The audience of students laughed. Principal Mayoral fidgeted in her seat and, like a coach whose player had fouled one time too often, got ready to bench Colin.

"We used to go wherever we could find a spot. Behind a tree." The slide pictured a little kid going behind a tree. The crowd of kids laughed.

"Behind a rock." He clicked to another slide of a kid's head behind a rock with an arc of water spraying over into view.

"What, you may wonder," Colin continued, looking out to the crowd, "did prehistoric men and women use before toilet paper came along?" His slide now showed a big prehistoric club with a roll of toilet paper overlaying it. His next slide was a pile of rocks.

"That's right, rocks." The students all laughed and moaned. "Leaves, wood chips, who knows what else?" he said, shrugging.

"I know what else," he answered his own question. "Later, as we became more evolved, we used corn cobs." A slide of a corn cob.

The students all moaned and laughed again.

"And later, these too." He clicked up an image of the Sears catalogue and a pile of newspapers.

"Somewhere between the rocks and that hard place, the Chinese began to use toilet paper in like 105 CE! But only the Emperor." A slide of an ancient portrait of a Chinese Emperor with the words, "The Emperor Liked His Throne" above the artwork.

That made the kids laugh too. Colin looked over at Mrs. Mayoral and continued.

"It wasn't until the 1800s that toilet paper was on a real roll. Ha, get it!?" No one laughed. "A real roll . . ." Colin repeated, and the audience of students groaned at his bad pun.

"Did you know," Colin continued, "that there were splinters in the paper until 1935 though? Do I need to tell you why splinters in toilet paper would be a bad thing?" A picture of a finger with a splinter accompanied this uncomfortable fact.

Now the students really groaned.

"Anyway," he went on, "you probably never think about it, but we should all be very thankful for the toilet paper that we have today."

Mrs. Mayoral crossed her legs and settled further back in her chair.

"And now, some toilet paper fun facts:

- We use about fifty-seven sheets of toilet paper a day.
- It takes about 384 trees to make the toilet paper that you will use in your lifetime.
- The average person uses 100 rolls of toilet

paper per year—over 20,000 sheets!
- The daily production of toilet paper is about eighty-three million rolls per day.
- The Cloud Nine paper mills alone now produce enough two-ply tissue to wrap around the Earth's circumference one and a half times—every day! That's 24,901 miles!

"That's a lot of matzah balls." He was getting silly, a sure sign he should wrap it up. Dewey gave him the cue to do so.

"So, now you have the facts. We should be grateful for toilet paper." Colin clicked to a slide of himself holding a roll and smiling big.

Something about Colin, with his big goofy grin while holding a roll of toilet paper seemed to bring out hysterics from the crowd.

Mrs. Mayoral stood up. "Okay, Colin. If that's all—"

"Oh! Just some important concluding words please, Mrs. Mayoral.

"Principal Mayoral, fellow students, here is my proposal regarding what some thoughtful geniuses have referred to as the t-issue—and it involves math, which I figure Mr. Peters will like. Let's work together. The school can share how many cases of toilet paper we use per month.

"Then . . ." Colin looked over, and Dewey gave him the hurry-it-up sign again, this time more emphatically, so he began to talk much faster. "Then we calculate how much the average person uses, and when we know how much we use, we can work to reduce it ourselves. Give us a goal we can work toward. Help us learn to waste less of this precious resource, in school and out! Let us be our own toilet paper roll monitors instead of that stupid gizmo that just makes me late for class."

He'd said it all in almost one long breath.

"Thank you for your consideration and time on this very important t-issue."

The crowd of students went wild with applause and cheers.

Mrs. Mayoral gave Colin a congratulatory nod as he sat back down in the audience. He could feel that his cheeks were still warm from his talk.

"Nice work," spoke Seraphina.

Dewey gave him a solid pat on the back.

"Well, *this* is taking longer than we had anticipated, and we certainly want to be sure to hear from other voices. We will take our scheduled nutrition break and meet back here in lieu of period four class. I'll dismiss you by sections."

Everyone filed out of the gymnasium, and now they could hear a buzz like the whole hive was alive.

"I wonder, though," said Colin, "if I get pegged for vandalism, do they have toilet paper in jail?"

"Ha!" laughed Dewey. "I'll ask Clara to bake you a cake. I wonder if anyone else is going to volunteer to speak?"

"You think?" asked Seraphina.

"Why not?" Dewey dropped an apple chip into his mouth.

They ate their snacks on the bench while kids came up to Colin and gave him high fives. He just shrugged when they asked if he'd put up the signs.

"I see no reason to give myself up."

"Nooo," agreed Seraphina and Dewey.

In fact, when the meeting began, another student did volunteer to speak. Olivia Portapath, the big league burper, raised her hand. To look at Olivia you'd never know that her small frame carried some gene that enabled her to extend a burp longer than your average soda burp contest winner. "My, oh my, that girl can sure repeat the morning news!" Clara proclaimed when she'd heard her once. Olivia Portapath really could let one rip.

Olivia went up to the microphone. "I wanted to say that I'm frustrated because we worked so hard on the garden, and now it's been kind of, well, desecrated."

Desecrated? Dewey and Seraphina looked at one another. The room got very quiet.

"I just don't think it's right," continued Olivia, "to hang all that stuff. How are the plants going to grow if there are cookies and chips all over the place?" Her wide eyes, once pools of stagnation in Mr. Nisano's class, now flickered with light.

The room started to get louder with students talking to one another. Dewey couldn't figure out if they agreed with Olivia or not.

"Quick," Dewey urged. "We gotta go up."

"Well," began Seraphina speaking as they both stood and walked up to the microphone area without raising their hands first. "We have some thoughts about that."

Julia stepped up to the mic and looked at Olivia for approval. Olivia nodded.

"Go ahead," offered Julia, stepping back again.

"Can we dim the lights again, please, Mrs. Mayoral?" Seraphina continued. "Like Colin, we think conservation is all about balance and moderation. The vending machine business does too."

They opened the first slide.

"Vending machines go all the way back to ancient Egypt. In 215 BCE, people paid with coins to dispense holy water."

They clicked to the next slide.

"When you think of vending machines, most people only think of candy, chips, and cookies, but vending machines can also have a lot of other stuff in them," narrated Seraphina.

Dewey went through the next few slides to show a picture of a camera, of pasta dinner, of fresh flowers, and t-shirts.

"And look at Japan! Grilled sandwiches, eggs, batteries, neckties, umbrellas! China even makes a giant car vending machine just for renting electric cars!" continued Dewey, changing the slide to show little green and white cars that looked like M&Ms. "For just a few dollars an hour!"

Seraphina read the next slide: "Balance." A variety of snacks made up the letters of the word. A celery stick and two round crackers made the letter "B," an apple formed the first "a," a banana stood in the place of the "l." A half-eaten cookie holding the letter "c" spot matched the nibbled peanut butter cup that formed the other "a." Sticks of jerky formed the "n," and the "e" was formed from with pretzel sticks.

"We, the students of Ladera Linda Middle School, would like to propose the following to the administration." They cued YouTube to Farmer Bacon's "Sundays," which had been Colin's eleventh hour contribution to their presentation, and his final redemptive act for all the trouble he had caused.

"Instead of getting *rid* of the vending machines, expand what you *put into* the vending machines."

The animated video clip of Farmer Bacon singing played:

Crackers and chips
They give you salty lips
So, don't fergit yer bananas

Cookies are nice
But so is brown rice
And bacon's always good on Sundays

Apples and cheese
And even celeries
Marshmallow pie's my fun day

Open the door
I'm going back for more
And bacon's always good on Sundays

The kids all joined in singing along with this educational video which many of them hadn't seen since preschool, and the auditorium was filled with the sound of their choral singing and laughter. After the video ended, Dewey had to wait for the peals of laughter to die down among the students.

"We propose," he continued, "creating a committee of students, parents, and teachers—oh, and you too, Mrs. Mayoral," Dewey added, craning his neck to look at her. "The committee will work together to select a *balance* of what goes in the vending machines. Some of the usual stuff and some of the healthy stuff."

"We propose to spend more time in health class discussing the healthy stuff that *we* kids like and will actually eat," said Seraphina.

The room of students applauded.

"We can still have our garden too!" added Seraphina. "And no, Olivia, I don't think that we—er, whoever—did that to the garden caused it any harm or meant to stop its progress. I think they just wanted to get this conversation started."

At that, Mrs. Mayoral stepped up to the podium.

"Um, we're not quite done yet," Dewey explained.

"Oh, I think you two are done," she replied with a look in her eye that was hard to read. "We're out of time. This has been quite well thought out. Give us your last thoughts, please."

Dewey forwarded to the final slide, an image of a vending machine with toilet paper rolls in it. "There won't always be little gizmos parceling out the toilet paper in life. We need to learn to make good choices."

The crowd cheered again. Dewey and Seraphina packed up and started to walk out of the gymnasium with the rest of the crowd for lunch, but Mrs. Mayoral approached them as they exited.

"After you've finished your lunches, come see me in my office. Please round up Colin on your way."

"Okay, Mrs. Mayoral," replied Dewey with a gulp.

Seraphina just nodded as they hurried away from the principal.

"You messed *up* when you almost let slip that *we* were in the garden!" ribbed Dewey once Mrs. Mayoral was out of earshot.

"I know, I know!" cringed Seraphina.

"Naw, don't worry about it," said Dewey. "She was bound to know it was us. No one else was even talking about the issue, let alone ready with presentations. He smiled. "It'll be okay. I think. There's Colin."

"Hey, Colin! We gotta go see Mayoral."

"It's okay. You two just go," he chuckled.

"Nice try," replied Seraphina. "Well, I can't eat. Let's just get it over with."

"Okay." Colin took a big bite of his sandwich. Evidently meeting with the principal didn't hurt his appetite.

"Split that with me?" asked Dewey.

"Sure, Buddy," said Colin, and he handed him half of his peanut butter and jelly sandwich.

Employee Vacation

That afternoon, before Dewey went home, he visited Clara to bring her up to speed and seek her advice.

They'd won the campaign at school, but each had been given detention for coming on campus after hours.

Mrs. Mayoral loved their ideas, loved their suggestions, but she said she'd be remiss not to hold them accountable for breaking such a serious rule and being on campus unchaperoned. Still, they'd gotten off easy and saved the school.

It had been a busy year for him so far, adjusting to a new school and taking on his new role as teacher problem solver. He'd had to figure out how to use a locker and juggle six different teachers with six different personalities. He felt maybe he and Clara hadn't spent as much time together as they once had, and he felt bad about it, even as he celebrated.

He wondered if maybe she felt bad about it too.

"So, sir, how progresses the Revolution?"

Clara stood about shoulder-height to Dewey and looked up at him as she pursued the details.

"The revolutionaries won!" he exclaimed. It felt so great to share the news with her, and she took it with such pleasure.

"Excellent news!"

Weird how it didn't seem to matter how little time he spent in this office or with Clara, they always fell right back into place. He needn't have worried, it seemed.

Wolfie heard the enthusiasm in their voices, and he dropped a new, rounded sheep toy at Dewey's feet. Wolfie's pink tongue hung, and his expressive eyes were full of expectation.

"Go get it!" Dewey called as he bounced the stuffed sheep across the room. Wolfie gave one solid bark and chased it.

"Dewey, do you think our clientele might be getting tired of cookies? I'm wondering if I should branch out a bit. Bake pies or cakes? Or maybe make small finger sandwiches . . ." proposed Clara.

"No! That's an awful idea, Clara! Why? Are you

tired of making cookies?" Dewey asked. He really hoped she'd say no.

"What? Me? Tired of cookies? No! There are thousands of types that I haven't even tried to make yet. I just wanted to make sure you didn't want things to evolve more around here."

"NO! No more changes. I like things just as they are," reassured Dewey.

Wolfie came back with his sheep smooshed up against his face. Deep into their conversation, neither Dewey nor Clara noticed. Wolfie waited and then, tired of waiting, threw it up in the air himself.

Dewey laughed and went to toss it, but, as usual, Wolfie grabbed and wouldn't release it, instead angling to play tug-of-war. Wolfie could also be counted on not to change too much, it seemed.

"Well, okay, then," Clara reassured back. "I would, however, like to discuss a vacation, Boss. You know, every employee gets one, and I haven't taken any vacation time since we started. I'm thinking since it's almost winter break, things might slow down around here, and I could go away for a bit. I'll leave you more cookies in the freezer. Just in case."

"Oh no," replied Dewey adamantly while tugging at the sheep firmly. "If you go, I'm shutting the office down until you're back. I'll take a break as well." He got the sheep from Wolfie's clench and tossed it across the room. "I can't run this place without you."

Clara's cheeks turned pink.

After a few moments playing with Wolfie, Dewey asked, "Where will you go on vacation?"

"Wolfie and I will go to the snow. He loves to play in the snow."

"Wow. Okay. I'll miss you both," said Dewey.

"We'll miss you as well, sir. I figure a month should do it."

"Huh. A vacation. Okay. Yeah. I guess we could all use that."

Clara gave Dewey a hug, and he gave her a warm hug back.

Drone On

Dewey's dad finished his first semester of being a student and a student teacher. This meant next fall he'd have a job as a full-fledged math teacher with classes of his own. If he worked at Ladera Linda, those classes would be keeping track of toilet paper use as part of their curriculum.

Dewey had managed to make it through his first semester of sixth grade. Toilet paper again rolled unfettered, and a new, improved pair of vending machines were on their way.

Today in the mail, he got the small drone his mom ordered for him a couple months ago. It had been on backorder, so Dewey had forgotten all about it!

Dewey's mom and dad sat on the couch watching some old TV show.

"Dad? You want to help me try out the drone? I finally got it charged."

"Sure!" He jumped up, running to the closet to get his tennis shoes. He tripped on a couch pillow that had fallen on the floor. Dewey's mom laughed at him.

"Don't trip over yourself, Don!"

"Where do you want to try her?"

"*Her*?" repeated Dewey.

"Well, in the military, they like to refer to ships and such as—"

"Dad!" *How come what was so funny with friends could be so annoying with parents?* Dewey wondered, rolling his eyes.

"Easy, *Turbo*!" said Dewey's mom as she rose to place her hand on Dewey's dad's shoulder.

"Oh, you guys don't know how to have any fun. Fine. Where would you like to fly *it?*"

"Greenblade Park?" suggested Dewey.

"Alright then! Let's take off!" said Dewey's dad as they walked out together.

"Oh, Dad!" groaned Dewey, and he heard his mom laugh from inside.

Dewey imagined Wolfie would love to run and chase the squirrels in this wide-open bowl of a field.

"Here's a good spot, Sport; what do you think?"

"Looks good."

Dewey tried launching the mini-drone, and it hovered but didn't take off well.

"Can I try?" asked his dad. "I think if you move the controls more this way . . ."

The drone took off and hovered high between the trees.

"Here you go, now just send it off," his dad said handing him back the controls.

"Cool!"

They took turns dipping and zipping the drone.

"Last time," Dewey shared, "Colin chased a butter-fly for a long time!"

"That's impressive," Dewey's dad sent the drone right over the top of Dewey's head.

"Hey!" laughed Dewey.

"Did you know," began Dewey's dad after some time had passed, "that the Pentagon is very interested in how mini-drones can study insects?"

"Really?"

"Oh, yeah. Insects, birds, fish, bats. All that stuff."

"The *Pentagon*? Why?"

"They want to maneuver through whatever envi-ronment may pose a challenge for them—the air, sea, deserts, forests, tall buildings in crowded cities. Animals manage it all the time. If they can get up close and study them, they learn how to navigate like a bat through the air or a fish through the water. And if humans can't do it, they'll invent robots programmed with the data they collect from the drones."

"Whoa. We never use Colin's for pictures," Dewey remarked. "We should figure that part out."

"That'd be cool," his dad agreed. "Get some lunch?"

"Yeah. It needs to be charged again anyway."

As they walked, Dewey's dad talked about the end of his semester. "I'm getting some nice cards this week, and kids said some pretty okay things. I think it went well overall, Dews."

Dewey felt relieved to hear that. It would be unfortunate if someone came to him with a teacher problem to solve about his own dad!

As they sat down to lunch, Dewey shared with him how he, Seraphina, Olivia, and Colin headed the new BC on CC—Balanced Conversations on Conservation Committee.

"Well, that's the name that the teachers suggested. We prefer D.U.H.—Don't Underestimate Humans. Picking a better committee name will be our first order of business when we get back."

The waitress delivered their burgers and fries to the table, as Dewey told him about the "T-ISSUE" and the vending machines. He brushed over some of the details which might've gotten him in trouble or exposed his undercover operation, but otherwise, he shared everything he and his friends had just lived to tell.

"Wait," his dad chewed and swallowed, putting down his burger. "You kids put up protest signs that said that?!" He wiped a spot of grease off his chin, thinking that he would order a salad in addition to his fries and burger. "That's clever, Dewey! Your mother is going to love that.

"You know, they say when you name your child after someone, you have to be careful because he might become that person himself one day. You know, like if you name a kid Darth, you're just asking for a killer, right?"

Dewey laughed and stuck a fry in his mouth, suddenly thinking about Clara's fry cookies. Too bad he couldn't tell his dad about those.

"We named you Dewey, and you went right out and showed them what a real democratic education looks like."

Dewey's dad texted his mom the proud news.

Dewey wasn't exactly sure what his dad meant, and he wasn't about to ask for fear of getting one of his long, trademark parent-life-talks. But he knew this—he and his dad sat sharing a burger and fries, enjoying the warm

California December day. Somewhere, Wolfie and Clara would be enjoying the snow. *Balance*, thought Dewey— and he ordered a hot fudge sundae.

About the Author

Lorri Horn is the author of the Kirkus starred novel *Dewey Fairchild, Parent Problem Solver*, which was listed as one of the Best Middle-Grade Books of 2017 by Kirkus Reviews.

Lorri spent her childhood days in California and has been working with kids all her life. She got her first babysitting job when she was nine years old, became a camp counselor, and went on to be a teacher.

Fascinated by the origins of behavior, Lorri spent a few years studying cercopithecus aethiops (vervet monkeys) and thought she'd become a famous biological anthropologist. But it turns out there's a decent amount of camping involved in that career. Plus, while it was fascinating to study and observe our little non-human primate brothers and sisters, Lorri found it much more rewarding to share a good book with a kid. Not once did those vervets gather round for story-time.

So Lorri became an educator and an author for humans, who, admittedly, sometimes monkey around. She has a degree in English, a teaching credential, has been Nationally Board Certified, and has taught public school for over 14 years.

She loves cheese (if she had to choose between cheese and chocolate on a deserted island, she'd have to say cheese—and that's saying a whole lot, because she's not sure how'd she live without chocolate), humor, baking, books, and spending time with her husband, son, and their dog—you guessed it—Wolfie.

Dewey isn't just good with parents, he's great with them!
But his biggest case may be his own.

DEWEY FAIRCHILD
PARENT PROBLEM SOLVER

Attic, 5555 Franklin Way / (c) 555-555-3399
Dewey@DeweyFairchild.com
By appointment only

LORRI HORN

Enjoy this sneak peek of how it all began.

One of Dewey's favorite new computer games involved simply clicking for cookies. The more you clicked, the more cookies you collected.

"Arrrgh! My arm is burning! I'm up to 8,000 cookies," yelled out Dewey's friend Colin while they each clicked away one day in the computer lab during lunch. "I'm going to get carpet tunnel!! But I don't care! Must. Get. 9,000!"

"Shh! Carpal tunnel, you goof. You need to buy more grandmas and farms, so they can make cookies for you."

"What I need is a little brother or one of those Harry Potter house elves I can command to click for me."

"Ha! Oh! I'm at 12,000!" Dewey announced.

Colin Decker stood about fifty-four inches tall, with brown eyes, brown skin, and curly black hair. That made him half an inch taller than Dewey, three-and-a-half times the height of a bowling pin, seven-tenths the height of Michael Jordan, one-fifth the height of a giraffe, one-sixteenth the height of a giant sequoia tree, one-seventeenth the height of the Statue of Liberty, and about 10,000 times the height of a sheet of paper.

Or so Colin had read online. You can't believe everything you read, though. So one of these days, before he grew too much, he planned on testing some of these out.

"Holy narwhal! My grandmas are losing their teeth."

Dewey laughed. Colin was obsessed with narwhals, those great whales of the arctic whose males grew up to sixteen feet long and had a single, gigantic tusk, like a unicorn, up to ten feet in length.

Grandmas, on the other hand, needed steel plated rolling pins to stand up to the great forces of nature. Or so it seemed.

This was the scene when their other lunch pal, Seraphina, shared a problem, and Dewey really had nothing better to do than help her (they really weren't supposed to be playing games in the lab). Plus, she always had good snacks, and he always felt hungry.

"I just can't take one more single day of it. My mother is a complete nut job. You *have* to help me!"

Seraphina Johnson was definitely flipping out. She came right at him, her books piled up under her lunch tray, the cheese sliding off of her pizza boat as her tray took a shortcut down her science book, and the juice from her fruit cup sloshed all over her fries.

"Um, watch your lunch!" Dewey cried as the tray slid off, narrowly missing the computer table and falling right into his hands. He wiggled the cheese back into place and balanced the tray on his knee.

"What!?" he asked, sucking the grease off of his fingers as Seraphina shot him a look for poking at her cheese.

She grabbed her lunch back, and they all headed out to the lunch tables.

"She's insane, that's what. Do you know that she still holds my hand when we cross the street?! When we got to school today, she actually parked the car, walked me in, and held my hand until we got to the other side." Seraphina moved her hair out of her face, sat down, and stared at them for a reply.

Dewey and Colin sat across from her at the tables, and Dewey took a bite of his peanut butter and jelly sandwich. There was just nothing about a school lunch that looked appetizing to him. Too much sauce on the pizza. Too much cheese. Seraphina didn't seem to be enjoying it much either as she went on and on about her mother. At least she hadn't taken a bite. Nothing not to like about the fries though; he reached over and grabbed a few that seemed to have escaped the puddle of fruit slosh.

Dewey's mom had made his sandwich. He knew because it was cut in triangles, not in half, which was his dad's style. He liked triangles better—much more satisfying biting into the corners. And what's up with the crust anyway? Why wouldn't his parents cut it off? It couldn't be healthier to eat the crust just because it's darker, right? Were there more minerals or vitamins in the crust? It didn't make any sense.

"Are you listening to me?!" Seraphina let go of her

long, brown, curly hair, which she'd been twisting while carrying on about her mother's overprotective ways. He was pretty sure he'd caught *most* of what she'd said.

Chips or pretzels were a must with PBJ, because the salt mixed with the sweetness of the jelly was epic. He wanted to say so but didn't want to seem insensitive to the plight of his fellow parent-sufferer.

"Maybe I can help," he said, pushing a chip and then a french fry into his mouth. "Let me follow you guys around a bit when your mom doesn't know and see if I can figure out what the fruit is going on."

Fruit. That had reminded him. He had a juicy nectarine in his lunch sack.

Colin, who had been mostly bored by the theatrics and lost in his own thoughts, looked up from his lunch. "Wait, what?" he said. Now *this* was going to be interesting.

**Find out what happens next in
*Dewey Fairchild, Parent Problem Solver***